No joking matter

"Oh, brother. One last thing. If you see any uauthorized monkeys lurking around, I want to know about it." Drover let out a giggle. "What's so funny?"

"It's a joke, right? Tee hee. We don't have monkeys around here."

"Drover, it's no joke. This particular monkey is a burglar. If he shows up, we've got problems. Any more questions?"

"What does he look like?"

"Who?"

"The monkey."

"How should I know? He looks like a monkey. If you see a monkey that looks like a monkey, it'll be a monkey. At that point, you come and tell me you've seen a monkey."

He stared at the ground and gnawed on his lip. "Let's see here . . . if I see a monkey that looks like a monkey . . . I think I've got it."

The Case of
the Monkey Burglar

HANK
THE COWDOG

John R. Erickson

Illustrations by Gerald L. Holmes

Maverick Books, Inc.

MAVERICK BOOKS, INC.
Published by Maverick Books, Inc.
P.O. Box 549, Perryton, TX 79070
Phone: 806.435.7611
www.hankthecowdog.com

First published simultaneously by Viking Children's Books and Puffin Books,
members of Penguin Putnam Books for Young Readers, 2006.
Currently published by Maverick Books, Inc., 2015.

1 3 5 7 9 10 8 6 4 2

Maverick Books, Inc. ISBN 978-1-59188-148-3

Hank the Cowdog® is a registered trademark of John R. Erickson.

Printed in the United States of America

For John and Jane Graves

CONTENTS

An Interesting
Visitor

It's me again, Hank the Cowdog. At first glance there was nothing about the vehicle that made it stand out. It was a red Chevy car with . . . I don't know, four doors and four tires. No big deal, except that it had come onto my ranch without permission, so Drover and I gave it the usual treatment.

We shifted into the Launch All Dogs Procedure, went ripping up the hill, and barked the car all the way down to the machine shed.

There, I waited to see if the driver would dare to step out. Sometimes they don't, you know. After they've seen all the amassed forces of the ranch's Security Division, sometimes they just sit in the car, afraid to move. But this guy seemed pretty

1

brave, and when he climbed out of the car, I understood why.

He was a deputy sheriff. On his belt he carried a pistol, two sets of handcuffs, and all that other stuff they load onto their belts. And you know what else? I knew the guy: Chief Deputy Kile of the Ochiltree County Sheriff's Department.

Do you remember Deputy Kile? He helped me solve the Case of the Saddle House Robbery . . . or I helped him. I don't remember all the details, but we worked the case together and sent a sneaking little saddle thief to the slammer.

Are you familiar with the word "slammer"? Maybe not, because it's one of the technical words we use in the Security Business. It means "jailhouse," and we call it "slammer" because . . . well, because every jailhouse has a big iron door, and when you throw a crook in jail, you close the door behind him and it SLAMS.

So instead of calling it a jailhouse, we call it *the slammer*.

Maybe this is obvious, but the point is that Deputy Kile and I were in the same line of work, right? He happened to work for the sheriff's department and I happened to be Head of Ranch Security, but both of us enforced the law and were the sworn enemies of all crooks, crinimals, spies, snakes, scorpions, and night monsters.

I was very interested in finding out why he had come to the ranch. He wasn't the kind of fellow who made social calls or engaged in idle chatter, so when Slim came out of the machine shed to greet him, I stationed myself nearby and listened to their conversation.

After exchanging pleasantries and thoughts about the weather and pasture conditions, Deputy Kile said, "Slim, I need to borrow some air. I've got a slow leak in that right front tire."

A slow leak in his tire? That was all? What a bum deal. I had hoped for something more exciting. I mean, let's face it, in August things get a little dull around here.

Slim looked at the tire. "I can fix it with a plug, if you've got a few minutes."

Deputy Kile said he had time, so Slim jacked up the car, pulled off the tire, and found the source of the problem: a mesquite thorn.

He pulled it out with a pair of needle-nose pliers and held it up. "Where'd you find a mesquite thorn? There ain't a mesquite tree within twenty miles of here."

The deputy smiled. "That's pretty good detective work. The other day, I was working a case in the south part of the county—more than twenty miles from here. It was kind of interesting."

"Tell me about it while I fix your tire."

Deputy Kile sat down on a five-gallon bucket in the shade. "We got a call from a farmer, said he was missing some tools from his shop. I drove down and checked it out. In front of the shop, I found some good clear footprints in the dust."

"So did you catch the man?"

"That was the funny part. The robber was barefooted, and the prints weren't human."

Slim looked up from the tire. "What do you mean? He was from outer space?"

The deputy laughed. "No, probably from a zoo or a circus. They were monkey tracks."

"Monkey tracks! Now hold on a second. You think some feller trained a monkey to rob and steal?"

"That's the way it looks. There was a clear path of monkey prints all the way from the shop to some tire tracks about a hundred yards away, and no sign that the man ever got out of his vehicle. You've got to admit that's pretty smart."

Slim laughed and shoved a rubber plug into the hole in the tire. "Well, that beats it all."

"It's got us scratching our heads, I can tell you that. The first thing I asked the farmer was— 'Where were your dogs while all of this was going

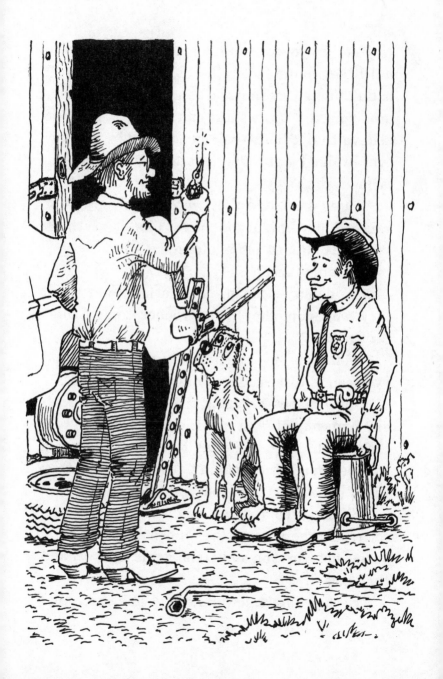

on?'"

Slim frowned, then his eyes prowled around until they found . . . well, ME, you might say. "I hadn't thought of that. I mean, Hank and Drover are about ten cards short of a full deck, but I do believe they'd bark their heads off if a monkey ever walked onto the place. Where *were* the farmer's dogs?"

"Three dogs, and they were all asleep . . . or *knocked out* might be more like it. I think somebody slipped 'em a mickey."

"A tranquilizer?"

The deputy nodded. "The farmer said when they woke up, they acted goofier than Cooter Brown."

"Well, I've never heard of such a thing, and I've been to three county fairs and four rodeos."

Slim finished plugging the tire, filled it with air, and mounted it on the car. Deputy Kile thanked him and offered to pay him for his trouble, but Slim wouldn't hear of it, so they shook hands and the deputy got back in his car.

"Slim, these thieves might still be in the area, so keep your eyes open for anything suspicious. Are you and Loper going to be around the place?"

"Heck yeah. I'm too broke to go anywhere, and

Loper's too cheap."

"Good. Let me know if you see anything."

The car pulled away, and Slim stood there for a moment, shaking his head. "Well, if that don't beat it all, a monkey burglar." He laughed to himself and went back to his welding job in the machine shed.

When he had gone, I turned to Drover, who was gazing up at the clouds. "Did you hear that?"

His eyes drifted down, and he gave me a grin. "Oh, hi. Did somebody just drive away?"

"Drover, that was the deputy sheriff and he was here for thirty minutes. You didn't hear anything he said?"

"Well, let's see. I heard something about . . . a tire. Did he have a tire on his car?"

I let out a groan. "Of course he had a car on his tire! He had four of them."

"He had four cars?"

"He had one car, four tires. Every car has four tires."

"How come?"

"Because every car has four wheels."

"Oh. What if one fell off?"

I gave him a withering glare. "Don't start this, Drover, I'm not in the mood for one of your loony conversations. Deputy Kile gave us a very interesting report about a gang of burglars, but it's obvious that you didn't hear any of it."

"They steal tires?"

"No, they don't steal tires. They steal tools. If you see a strange vehicle driving around, let me know at once."

"A vehicle with four tires?"

"Exactly."

"That wouldn't be strange. You said they all had four tires."

"Stop talking about tires! What's wrong with you?"

He grinned. "I don't know. All at once, I'm just . . . thinking about tires."

"Oh, brother. One last thing. If you see any unauthorized monkeys lurking around, I want to know about it." He let out a giggle. "What's so funny?"

"It's a joke, right? Tee hee. We don't have monkeys around here."

"Drover, it's no joke. This particular monkey is a burglar. If he shows up, we've got problems. Any more questions?"

"What does he look like?"

"Who?"

"The monkey."

"How should I know? He looks like a monkey.

If you see a monkey that looks like a monkey, it'll be a monkey. At that point, you come and tell me you've seen a monkey."

He stared at the ground and gnawed on his lip. "Let's see here . . . if I see a monkey that looks like a monkey . . . I think I've got it."

"Good. And in the future, I hope you'll try to . . ."

I had planned to give Drover a lecture on goofing off and not paying attention, but just then I heard footsteps approaching from the direction of the house. I turned and saw Loper plodding up the hill. Even at a distance, I could see that he was in a bad mood.

Since he owned the ranch and was more or less in charge of things, this wasn't particularly good news.

CHAPTER TWO

Loper and Sally May Go on a Vacation

When Our People are feeling angry or depressed, we dogs notice it right away, and a lot of times we can fix the problem.

When I saw Loper coming my way, with doom and gloom written all over his face, I trotted over to him. Flinging my tail back and forth in Happy Wags, I gave him a big smile that said, "Hey, Loper, great news. I'm here!"

With his eyes fixed on the ground, he walked right past and didn't even look at me. I mean, no "good morning" or "great to see you, Hank." Nothing. What a grouch.

He and his cloud of gloom disappeared inside the machine shed, and a moment later I heard the following conversation.

Loper: "I've got some bad news. Sally May wants to take a vacation."

Slim: "What's so bad about that?"

Loper: "Well, it's ridiculous. When you're in the ranching business, you can't just go waltzing off to the mountains. She wants us to go for a whole three days! We've got hay in the field, yearlings in the sick pen, fence to fix, windmills to check . . ."

Slim: "Did you explain all that to Sally May?"

Loper: "Of course I did."

Slim: "What did she say?"

Loper: "She said that we've never had a vacation."

Slim: "Huh. And what did you say to that?"

Loper: "I said that being married to me should be all the vacation a woman needs."

Slim: "Heh. How did that go over?"

Loper: "Like a snake in the bathtub."

They stepped out of the machine shed, and I could see that Slim was trying to bite back a smile. "Loper, I think you got it backwards. Any woman who'd stay married to you deserves a trip to the mountains. And a million bucks."

Loper gave him a sour look. "What do you know about women? The last time I checked, you were still a bachelor, and I haven't noticed any ladies lined up at your gate, trying to get in."

"They come during work hours when you're taking a nap."

"I mean, your life is so simple, it's pathetic. The only difference between you and a grasshopper is that you wear socks."

"I can sing too. That's a big difference."

"I've heard you sing. Even the dogs can't stand it."

Slim pulled a toothpick out of his hatband and slid it through his teeth. "Loper, just think of all the fun things you can do on vacation. Why, you can take Alfred fishing."

"That's fun? I'd rather clean out the septic tank."

"Well, go see a movie."

Loper rolled his eyes. "Do you know what it costs to take a family to a movie? A fortune, and they charge two bucks for a dinky little sack of popcorn."

"Take some sunflower seeds."

"I don't like sunflower seeds."

"Then take the kids to one of them water parks."

Loper glared at him. "Water! Do I need to drive three hundred miles to play in the water? We've got stock tanks all over this ranch, and two miles of creek."

Slim shook his head. "Loper, you make a mule

look reasonable. You do all this bellyaching, and what's the point? Tomorrow morning, you'll load up the car and drive to the mountains. You might as well be brave and have some fun."

Loper grunted. "I'll be brave, I'll load the car, I'll drive halfway across the country, and when I get there, I *won't* have fun."

"All right, don't have fun. Go to the mountains and pout for three days."

"I will."

"Good. I hope you're miserable, but I won't be." Slim flashed a smile. "When I get you off the place, I'm going to have a blast."

"Oh, yeah?"

"That's right. It'll be like three days without a rotten tooth."

"You really think so?"

Slim hitched up his jeans. "Yes sir, I know so."

Loper gazed off into the distance and was quiet for a moment. "You know, we've got eight hundred bales of hay in the alfalfa field."

Slim blinked. "Yeah, but..."

"I just had a great idea." Loper slid his gaze back to Slim. "While I'm gone, maybe you'd like to haul some hay."

Slim's Adam's apple jumped. "By myself?"

"You can take the dogs."

"Now, Loper . . ."

Loper flashed a grin. "See, that's one thing about bosses, Slim. We don't want the hired hands to be happy when we're gone."

"This ain't funny."

Loper let out a big laugh. "Sure it is. It's hilarious. While I'm miserable having fun, you'll be miserable hauling hay. It'll help ease my pain." Loper walked over to him and whispered, "Never let the boss know you're glad to see him go. It'll come back and bite you every time."

Chuckling to himself, Loper walked down to the house. Slim glared after him for a long time, then turned to me. "Me and my big mouth."

Right, and I could have told him, but do these guys ever listen to their dogs? No, and that's why we try to keep our opinions to ourselves.

The next morning around nine o'clock, Loper loaded Sally May and the children into the family car, and off they went to the mountains. I led them all the way up to the mailbox on the county road and sent them on their way with Barks of Farewell. That done, I made my way back to headquarters and went looking for Slim.

I had a feeling this was going to be a hard day, and he would need all the support we dogs could provide. I mean, he'd been tagged with a pretty tough assignment—hauling eight hundred bales of alfalfa hay all by himself.

On any ranch with modern equipment, that wouldn't have been such a difficult job, but our outfit did everything The Cowboy Way. That means we shunned all laborsaving devices and relied entirely on junk machinery.

See, we had only thirty acres of irrigated alfalfa, and that wasn't quite enough to justify the expense of good equipment. Loper bought all our machinery at farm auctions, and took considerable pride in getting what he called "good deals."

Ha. Those guys spent half their summers reading repair manuals, running to town for parts, turning wrenches, and screaming at gutted hay balers and swathers, whose parts lay scattered all over the floor of the machine shed.

But every now and then the machinery held together long enough to put up some of the hay into bales, and at that point they had to be hauled out of the field and unloaded in the "stack lot," an area that had been fenced off so that the cattle wouldn't plunder the hay and scatter it over half the ranch.

Under ordinary conditions, our hay-hauling involved the use of an old flatbed truck and three people: Sally May to drive the truck through the field; Slim to pitch the bales up on the truck; and Loper to stack the hay on the back of the truck.

Do you see what Slim had done with his big mouth? He would have to do all three of those jobs by himself. I felt some pity for poor Slim. I mean, slaving in a hay field in the heat of summer wasn't something I would wish on a friend, or even an enemy. On the other hand, he had walked into it with his mouth wide open and . . . well, what can you say?

Some people never learn, or if they learn, it has to be in the hardest possible way. Slim seemed to be one of those people. Now, if he had consulted his dogs, if he had listened to my advice . . . oh, well. We've already touched on that, and there's no more to be said.

The worst part of it was that we dogs would have to listen to him moan and gripe for three long days. It would a tough assignment for those of us in the Security Division, as we shared Slim's pain and eased him through this difficult period in his life. Drover and I would have our hands cut out for us.

When I returned to the yard gate, Slim wasn't there, but I found Drover making idle conversation with the cat. Pete.

When he saw me approaching the gate, Kitty

Kitty gave me one of his insolent smirks and said, "Well, well, Hankie the Wonderdog is here."

"You got that right, kitty. Out of the way." I pushed him aside and managed to step on his tail, tee hee, which wasn't exactly an accident. "Oops, sorry, Pete. If you'd find some other place to loaf, you wouldn't get stepped on." I marched up to Drover and gave him a stern glare. "What's going on around here?"

"Oh, hi. Are you talking to me?"

"Correct. What's going on around here?"

"Oh, not much. Pete and I were just talking about the weather."

"I see. And what did you decide?"

"Well, let me think." He rolled his eyes around. "I think we decided that it'll probably do whatever it does, and we'll just wait and see."

"That's very impressive, Drover."

"Thanks."

"How long did it take you and the cat to decide that the weather will do whatever it does?"

"Oh . . . about fifteen minutes, I guess. We argued about it for a while."

"How interesting."

"Yeah, Pete said it was going to be hot and dry, but I said it would be dry and hot. Then we decided we didn't know for sure."

"I see. Do I need to remind you that mingling with cats is against regulations?"

"Well, we weren't mingling. We were just talking."

Pete nodded. "That's right, Hankie, we weren't mingling."

"Stay out of this, kitty. This is dog business and nobody wants to hear what you have to say." Back to Drover. "You were mingling, and unless you can come up with a good reason for mingling with a cat, this will have to go into my report."

"Oh, darn. Well, let me think." He wadded up his face and seemed to be probing his tiny mind. "You know, I'm not real sure what 'mingle' means, but it rhymes with 'tingle.'"

"It rhymes with 'tingle,' but I don't care."

"And 'care' rhymes with 'underwear.'"

Pete's face lit up with a smile. "Good point, Drover! Why, with just a little imagination, we could compose a poem: 'We tingle as we mingle, but I don't care/'Cause Wonderdog Hankie lost his underwear.'"

Does this strike you as silly and childish? It did me, but there's more. Hang on while we change chapters.

CHAPTER THREE

An Important
Lesson in Poetry

If you recall, Pete the Barncat had composed a silly little poem. Do I dare repeat it? I guess it wouldn't hurt.

"We tingle as we mingle, but I don't care/'Cause Wonderdog Hankie lost his underwear."

See? I told you it was silly, but Drover burst out with a giggle. "Tee hee. Oh, that's a good one, Pete."

I marched over to the cat and gave him a snarl. "Okay, kitty, this has gone far enough. At this point, I have two words for you."

"Happy birthday?"

"No."

"Merry Christmas?"

"No."

"Great poem?"

"No. My two words to you are . . . shove off, get lost, and beat it!"

The cat fluttered his eyelids. "But Hankie, that's seven words. Maybe you miscounted."

"Oh, yeah? Then let me explain." I stuck my nose in his face and said, "ROOF!"

Heh heh. That got him. You should have seen the little pest. My Air Horns Bark blasted his ears off and sent him rolling backwards, hissing and spitting.

I love doing that. See, you have to be firm with these cats. When they start mouthing off, you don't argue with 'em or try to be reasonable. You give 'em Air Horns right in the face. That will settle most arguments with a cat. And it's great fun too.

Well, that took care of my business with the cat, so I marched back to my assistant. "Okay, where were we?"

"Well, let me see. I think you were talking about . . . poetry."

"Ah, yes. Poetry." I began pacing back and forth in front of him. "It's a very important subject, Drover, because we dogs take pride in our ability to compose verses. Cats try to cobble up a poem every now and then, but the result is always embarrassing."

"I thought it was pretty good."

"They have no talent for language."

"I liked the part about your underwear."

"They have no sense of meter or rhyme."

"I thought it was funny as heck."

I stopped pacing. "What?"

Drover glanced around. "I didn't say anything."

"I thought I heard a voice."

"I'll be derned. It wasn't me."

I looked up into a tree nearby. "Hmmm. It must have been a bird." I resumed pacing. "Dogs, on the other hand, seem to have a natural skill for composing delightful poems, and to demonstrate this, you give me a word and I'll make up a poem about it."

"Any word?"

"Any word at all. Give me your best shot."

"Well, let's see. 'Bulldozer.'"

I pitched that one back and forth in my mind. "Tell you what, let's try another one."

"'Pork rinds.'"

"That's two words, Drover. Try to play by the rules."

"Sorry. 'Leprosy.'"

I stopped in my tracks. "'Leprosy'! Who can make a rhyme with 'leprosy'?"

"Well, it's a word."

"It's not a word, it's a disease. Diseases don't count in this contest. Give me a normal, healthy American word."

He frowned. "Darn. Okay, here's one. 'Chrysanthemum.'"

"That's not an American word, it's Chinese."

He gave me a devilish grin. "Yeah, and I'll bet you can't write a poem about it."

I marched a few steps away and gazed off into the distance. Drover had challenged my gifts as a poet. Was I dog enough to accept the challenge, or would I wilt under the terrible stress of composing verses about chrysanthemums? This would likely be the most difficult poetic venture I had ever attempted, and the odds against success were astrometrical.

But my pride and reputation were at stake. I strode back to him and prepared to wipe that little smirk off his mouth. "All right, son, I accept your challenge."

He was stunned. I mean, when his eyes came up, they looked like two big moons with a fly in the center of each. "No fooling? You're going to do a poem about chrysanthemums?"

"Not just a poem, Drover. I'm going to raise the bar and make it even more difficult. I'm going to compose an entire *song* about chrysanthemums.

It's never been done before. Nobody has even dared to attempt it."

"Oh my gosh!"

And with Drover watching in stunned silence, I wrote, composed, arranged, and performed this song, surely one of the most spectacular of my entire career.

The Impossible Chrysanthemum Song

Chrysanthemum flowers are round like a
  ball.
They grow in the summer and bloom in the
  fall.
Sometimes they're yellow and sometimes
  they're not.
Chrysanthemums usually live in a pot.

If I were a flower, I'd want to announce
That I had a name normal folks could
  pronounce.
"Chrysos'" means gold if you happen to
  speak
That musty old language that came from
  the Greeks.

Chrysanthemum, chrysanthemum,

A word you can't say while you're
   chewing your gum.
This flower is pretty and pleasant to
   smell,
But, man, it is really a booger to spell.

If I took a notion to send a bouquet,
I'd pick out a flower whose name I could
   say.
See, what would you write, if you added a
   card?
"Herewith a flower, the name is too hard
To pronounce."

I think that chrysanthemums surely must
   be
The loneliest flowers you ever will see.
Why, even the insects avoid 'em too.
Four-syllable flowers are harder to chew.

   Chrysanthemum, chrysanthemum,
   A word you can't say while you're
      chewing your gum.
   This flower is pretty and pleasant to
      smell,
   But, man, it is really a booger to spell.

One more thing 'bout chrysanthemum's
    name:
It's certain to drive all the poets insane.
Try it yourself and give it some time,
But you'll never invent a chrysanthemum-
    rhyme.

A song 'bout this flower's impossible to
    make.
Shakespeare himself would have gotten
    the shakes.
Brave poets who tried it are now on the
    shelf,
But Drover, take note: I've done it myself!

    Chrysanthemum, chrysanthemum,
    A word you can't say while you're
        chewing your gum.
    This flower is pretty and pleasant to
        smell,
    But, man, it is really a booger to spell.

Pretty awesome song, huh? You bet. Even I
was amazed. I turned to Drover and waited for
him to burst into applause. He didn't.

    "Hey, I just performed a song about
chrysanthemums. Do you suppose you could show

some respect?"

"Well, it was pretty good, I guess."

"Pretty good? Drover, it's never been done before. This was a first."

"Yeah, but you didn't really make a rhyme with chrysanthemum."

"'Gum.' 'Gum' rhymes with 'mum.'"

He grinned. "Yeah, but that's kind of like cheating. I thought you were going to make a rhyme with the whole word."

"Drover, there is no word that will rhyme with 'chrysanthemum,' and in case you missed it, that was the whole point of the song."

"Well . . . I liked Pete's poem better."

"You . . . what?" I stormed away from the little goof. "Just skip it, Drover. I'm sorry I bothered. Your mind is sick and there's nothing we can do about it."

"Where are we going?"

"Don't speak to me."

"Are you looking for Slim?"

"Yes."

"You're going in the wrong direction."

I whirled around and reversed directions. "Don't tell me what to do, and stop following me. Someone might think we're friends."

You see what I have to put up with? The little

dunce liked Pete's pitiful little verse about underwear better than my tribute to . . . oh well.

I found Slim behind the machine shed, scowling at the motor of the old truck. It had been parked there since our last hay-hauling experience, a month ago. The hood was up, and Slim had reached his hand down toward the motor.

I knew what was coming next, and came to a sudden stop. Drover ran into me. "Oops, sorry. Oh look, there's Slim."

"Right. Listen, Drover, I've got a little job for you."

His face lit up. "Oh, goodie. You mean we're friends again?"

"Why yes, of course. That little spat we had about poetry . . . well, in the larger scheme of things, it meant nothing, almost nothing at all."

"Oh, good. There for a minute, I thought you were mad at me."

I gave a careless laugh. "Friends argue, Drover, but friendship remains the same."

"Yeah, like pork rinds."

"Pork rinds?"

"Yeah, they're always the same. Greasy. They give me indigestion."

"Yes, of course." I leaned toward him and

whispered, "Drover, Slim's having a bad day. I think one of us should rush over to him and . . . you know, cheer him up with Howdys and Happy Looks. Which of us could do that?"

He puzzled over that for a moment, then his face broke into a wide grin. "You know what? I think I could do it."

"No kidding?"

"Yeah, 'cause I'm in a happy mood, and I know how to do Howdys."

"With your stub tail?"

"Oh, yeah, I can wiggle it fast. See?" He gave me a demonstration of wiggling his tail. It was pathetic, but I pretended to be impressed.

"That's perfect, Drover, just what he needs. Okay, pal, rush over there and do your stuff. I'll be right here, cheering you on."

"Okay, here I go!"

Heh heh. Do you see what's coming? You'll love it.

CHAPTER FOUR

Naptime on the Prairie

The timing on this deal couldn't have been better. Drover rushed over to Slim and started wig-wagging his tail. Slim pulled out the dipstick, squinted at it, and began looking around for a grease rag on which to wipe it.

Now do you see what's coming? Tee hee. I didn't wish to be cruel to the runt, but let's face it. Most of the time it was MY ear that got used as a grease rag, and I didn't figure it would hurt Drover to be pressed into service. He would get a dirty ear, but so what?

One of Drover's problems is that he stays clean all the time. Show me a dog who never gets dirty and I'll show you . . . something. A dog who has missed out on many of Life's Richest Moments.

It was for his own good, see, and it also served him right for making a mockery of my Poetry Lesson.

The stage was set. Slim glanced around for something on which to wipe his dipstick, and there was little Drover at his feet—earnest, sincere, happy, cheerful, and dumb.

"Hank!" Slim called.

Huh?

"Come here!"

Me? There must have been some mistake. I mean, we had already made arrangements for Drover to do the job, right?

"Come here, pooch. I need a big floppy ear for this, and yours is about the size of a tortilla."

A tortilla! Why, I had never been so insulted! And what did the size of my ear have to do with it anyway? I mean, any moron could clean a dipstick on . . .

"Hurry up, you're burning daylight."

I couldn't believe it. He was serious about this; he wasn't kidding. This was an outrage!

Okay, have we discussed the problem with Drover's ears? Maybe not, but we should. See, he had a rinky-dink set of ears, not a big manly set like mine, and when our cowboys needed to borrow an ear for an important job, naturally they, uh, came to me. Drover's ears flunked the test.

So when the call came for me to step forward and offer my ear in selfless service to the ranch, I was filled with pride. Slim had picked the right dog and made a wise decision. Holding my head at a proud angle, I marched forward, elbowed Mister Squeakbox out of the way, and offered my ear for the greater glory of the ranch.

Slim took my ear and folded it in half. "Heck, if a guy had some guacamole and cheese, he could build a pretty nice burrito."

I tried to ignore him. Slim wants to be a comedian when he grows up, but some of us have doubts that he'll ever grow up. And it's no secret that his jokes are stale and corny.

A little humor there, did you catch it? Corny. Tortillas are made of corn, see? Ha ha. Okay, maybe it wasn't so great, but it was better than Slim's stale humor.

I didn't mind lending my ear to The Cause, but I didn't appreciate him saying that my ear was as big as a TORTILLA. It wasn't. My ears have a very pleasant shape, and you don't have to take my word on that. Ask any lady dog in Texas. They know great ears when they see them, and they've always gone nuts about mine.

Anyway, I did my loyal service to the ranch, ignored Slim's childish jokes, and stood there whilst he pulled the dipstick through the fold of my ear. That done, he scrubbed his fingernails on the other ear and patted me on the chest so hard that it made me cough.

HARK!

"Thanks, pooch. You're a true hero, I don't care what everybody says."

At that point, I turned to Drover, who was still hopping around like a cricket and wearing a loony grin. Oh, and he was squeaking, "Happy, cheerful, happy, cheerful!"

"You can shut it off, Drover. The show's over."

"How'd I do? Did I cheer him up? Boy, that was fun."

My lips formed a snarl, and I found myself wondering . . . how does he always manage to weasel out of the dirty jobs? If it happened once or twice, you might not think anything about it, but this happens over and over.

Oh well.

The important thing is that Slim had managed to check the oil in the truck, and he was ready to move on to the next step. He climbed into the cab, pumped the gas pedal, pulled out the choke, and hit the starter. The motor cranked and groaned, and finally started, sending a plume of blue-and-white smoke through the cab.

See, it didn't have a muffler or tailpipe, so all the exhaust smoke came straight out of the maniflubber . . . whatever you call that thing . . . and it fumed up the cab so badly, Slim vanished inside a blue cloud. Now and then I caught sight of his hands flapping the smoke around, and I could hear him coughing.

He left the motor running and went into the machine shed for his hay chaps, hay hooks, water jug, and sack lunch. When he returned, he pitched me and Mister Happy up into the seat and pointed a bony finger at the paper sack.

"That's my lunch. Don't even think about getting into it."

Me? Steal his lunch? Why, such a wicked thought had never . . . sniff sniff . . . by George, it did smell pretty good.

"Hank, get your nose out of my lunch!"

Sure, fine. I was just . . . boy, friendship sure doesn't count for much on this outfit, not when there's a scrap of food involved.

He threw the truck into first gear, and we were off to the hay field. Over the roar of the motor, Slim yelled, "She's kind of loud, ain't she?"

Yes, loud and smoky. Cough.

We drove north to the county road, turned right, and followed it east for a mile to the alfalfa patch. There, we left the main road and drove out into the field, whose surface was lined with row after row of hay bales. Eight hundred of them.

Slim stopped the truck and gazed out at the field. "You know, when a guy's driving down the road and sees a bunch of hay on the ground, it looks kind of pretty. But it changes things when he knows he has to load and stack every stinking bale."

We all climbed out of the truck. Slim strapped on his hay chaps to protect his legs from the scratchy hay, pulled on a pair of leather gloves, and seized a hay hook in each hand. Then he went to work.

Have we gone over the procedures for loading and hauling hay? Maybe not, so let's take a quick review. When one man is doing the job, he parks the truck beside one of the lines of bales and loads up the ones that are within easy walking distance, usually five or six bales.

With a hay hook in each hand, he stabs the hooks into the ends of a bale and lifts it up to his thighs. Holding the bale against his legs, he carries it to the truck and throws it up onto the flatbed. After he has loaded five or six bales, he climbs up onto the bed of the truck and stacks the bales, two across and one longways. Then he drives the truck forward and repeats the process.

After he's done this about ten times, he's got a load on the back of the truck, three or four bales high. He drives the truck back to headquarters, throws the bales off on the ground in the stack lot, and starts building a big haystack that will remain in the lot until we feed it to the cattle over the winter.

Then it's back to the field for another load. Over and over, all day. Whew! Just talking about it makes me hot and thirsty. See, what you have to remember is that there's no shade in a hay field, and by noon, the temperature might be up in the high nineties or even over a hundred degrees.

Oh, I almost forgot to mention that while Slim was loading and stacking the hay, we dogs had our own work to do. Every time he picked up a bale, we had to be cocked and ready to dive on any mice or rats that had taken up residence beneath the bale, so don't get the idea that Slim was the only one working his tail off.

Mousing is a very demanding job, and it requires a specialized kind of tail-work that most dogs don't even know about. See, before Slim picks up a bale, we have to be in the Lock-and-Load Position, whipping our tails back and forth to let him know that we're ready to pounce on whatever dangerous beasts might be lurking under there.

Sometimes it's just crickets or beetle bugs, but sometimes it's a field mouse or even a huge pack rat. Pack rats are a special challenge, don't you see, because they not only can run, hide, and dive into holes, but if you happen to grab one, he'll whip around and bite your lip off.

For that reason, we . . . uh . . . sometimes find it convenient to let the pack rats escape. I mean,

who wants to go through life without lips? Those lips are pretty important. Without lips, you can't whistle, smile, pout, or deliver flaming kisses to lady dogs, and who needs that? So, yes, we had developed a special set of procedures for dealing with pack rats.

We pretty muchly left 'em alone, if you want to know the truth.

Anyhow, that's today's lesson on loading, stacking, and hauling hay. It's pretty impressive that a dog would know so much about the hay business, isn't it?

You bet.

Now, where were we? Oh, yes, in the cool of morning we hauled four loads of alfalfa to the stack lot, and by then the heat had moved over the hay field like a heavy blanket. A white ball of sun blazed down on us from a cloudless sky, and there wasn't a breath of wind. Slim had dripped enough sweat to fill a fair-sized bucket, and he was looking a little wilted.

He poured some water down the back of his shirt and fanned his face with his hat. "If Loper was here, he'd crack the whip and we'd keep a-going, but you know what?" He grinned down at us dogs. "He ain't here. I finally got him off the ranch, and now I'm going to take me a big old juicy nap." He frowned. "Wait, hold everything. Have I sung you dogs my special deluxe nap-taking song?"

Drover and I exchanged looks of dread. Oh no, another of his ridiculous songs! Could we stand another one? It was too late for us to run and hide, so we put on our bravest faces and prepared to listen to the tiresome thing. Here's what he sang.

Naptime on the Prairie

There's many a story 'bout old-timey
  cowboys
That tell of both famine and feast.
They drove herds of cattle to Dodge City,
  Kansas,
And put 'em on trains to the East.

They crossed 'em through mountains and
  valleys and deserts,
And drove 'em through blizzards and sleet.
From daylight to darkness, those heroes
  pushed on
And rarely had chances to sleep.

Well, it's naptime on the prairie,
When a cowboy's ambition grows dim.

In the heat of the day,
It's just normal to lay
In the shade of a cottonwood limb.

A modern cowpuncher who works on a
  ranch
Has adapted on different lines.
With inside commodes and gravel-packed
  roads,
He's missed out on lots of good times.

There's much that he missed but things
  that he's gained
In being a hundred years late.
See, now when the boss drives away from
  the ranch,
The cowpuncher heads for the shade.

Well, it's naptime on the prairie,
When a cowboy's ambition grows dim.
In the heat of the day,
It's just normal to lay
In the shade of a cottonwood limb.

Those 'punchers who lived in the great
  golden days
Never thought about grabbing a nap.

Or maybe they did and just didn't tell it
To grandchildren perched on their lap.

They say that those trail-driving cowboys
    were tougher
Than those of us living today.
I really don't care, as I pull up a chair
And take me a nap in the shade.

Well, it's naptime on the prairie,
When a cowboy's ambition grows dim.
In the heat of the day,
It's just normal to lay
In the shade of a cottonwood limb.

In the heat of the day,
It's just normal to lay
In the shade of a cottonwood limb.

CHAPTER FIVE

The Guppy Invasion

Well, there you have it, Slim's deluxe nap-taking song, and I must admit that it wasn't as bad as some of the other duds he'd inflicted on us. Actually, it was pretty good. I mean, it had a melody and it even rhymed in spots, so maybe he was getting better with practice.

But I would be less than honest if I didn't point out a pretty serious mistake in the chorus. Out in the middle of the hay field, Slim didn't have a "cottonwood limb" to make shade. Would you like to guess where he found his shade?

He crawled under the truck. There, he made a pillow of his hay chaps and uttered a growl of contentment. "Dogs, if somebody comes along and tries to steal my truck, give me a bark. Otherwise, keep your traps shut, and I'll see you in about half an hour."

Steal his truck? Who would . . . okay, it was a joke. There wasn't a thief in the whole state of Texas who would have bothered to steal such a heap of junk, so we sure didn't have to worry about that.

And as for me keeping my trap shut . . . fine. What did he think I was going to do, run around and waste a bunch of good barking in the heat of the day, while he sawed logs under the truck?

Forget that, Charlie. He wasn't the only employee of the ranch who deserved a nap. There was someone called ME, and I already had my eye on a nice piece of shade under the . . .

"Not under here, bozo."

. . . a nice piece of shade on the north side of the truck, shall we say. I did my Three-Turns-Around-the-Bed and collapsed. It didn't bother me one bit that Slim had hogged the best shade under the truck.

Okay, it kind of hurt my feelings, and my name wasn't "Bozo."

Who is Bozo, anyway? Slim called me that all the time, and I had a feeling that there was some kind of joke behind it, but I didn't know the whole story. I made a mental note to ask around and find out who this Bozzzzzzzzzzzzzzz . . .

Bozo wozo, flibbering flozo . . . meek wonk whippersnapper whickerbill . . . mudpie pigpen honkly snork sniff . . . zzzzzzt . . . Beulah riding in a cricket wicket . . . red balloon wheedle wheelbarrows . . . zzzzzzzzzzzzzzzzzzz.

You think I wasn't worn-out, exhausted? Hey, all that work on Mouse Patrol had pretty muchly drained my tank, and once I hit that piece of shady ground, fellers, my lights went out. Exhaustion overwhelmed me, and I tumbled down the deep hole of sleep.

It was delicious sleep, wonderful sleep, the kind of sleep that ravels up the knitted sleeve of . . . something. It was great sleep, the kind of healing sleep that every Head of Ranch Security longs for and . . .

"Hank?"

. . . deserves.

"Hank?"

Huh? I heard a voice . . . a voice from outside the deep well of sleep . . . a voice that seemed to be calling someone's name.

"Hank, you'd better wake up."

Hank? Who was Hank? Did I know anyone named Hank? Did I have a name? Guppy-thoughts swam through the aquarium of my mind. Yes, I had a name: Flibbering Flozo. The call wasn't for me.

Zzzzzzzzzzzzzzzz.

"Hank, somebody's here!"

Suddenly I felt myself being launched up the dark well of sleep, scattering guppy-thoughts and guppy-dreams in all directions. I leaped to my feet and . . . BONK . . . almost broke my head on the stupid running board of the . . .

I blinked my eyes and swayed back and forth on rubber legs. There, standing right in front of me, I saw . . . four little white dogs! No, wait, two little white dogs.

Huh? Okay, one little white dog. "Drover? Is that you I see before me?"

"Well, I don't know if I'm before or after, but it's me."

"Good. Great. I've called this meeting of the Security Division to discuss . . ." I staggered three steps to the right and collapsed. I found myself staring at the dirt. It looked exactly like dirt, only more so. "Drover, how long has it been like this?"

"Like what?"

"I'm not sure. I was hoping you might know." I blinked my eyes and glanced around. "Where are we?"

Drover grinned. "We're in the alfalfa field."

"Yes, of course." I staggered to my feet and tried to put on a solemn face. "I've called this meeting to discuss alfalfa. Do you have anything to report?"

He stared at me. "Well, it's kind of like hay."

"Good. Excellent report. Now we're ready to vote. Everyone in favor of alfalfa, open your mouth and say 'ahhhh.'"

"Ahhhhh."

All at once, I noticed that Drover's mouth was open. "Did you just open your mouth and say 'ahhhhhh'? Are you sick? Do you think I'm a doctor? What's wrong with you, Drover?"

"I'm not sure."

"Did you see all those fish? There were hundreds of little fish, Drover. Guppies."

"I was a guppy once."

"You were a puppy."

"Maybe that was it, but I played in the water."

"Drover, somebody drained the tank. All the fish are gone. Only moments ago, there were all these fish inside the aquarium and . . ." I gave my head a shake and moved closer to Drover. "Did I say something about fish?"

"Yeah. I think they were muppies."

"Hmmm. Listen carefully. All references to fish will be stricken from the record, do you understand? It was all a big mistake, a breakdown in communications. There were no fish."

"Got it."

"Now, one last question. Did you just wake me up?"

"Well, I tried."

I heaved a big sigh. "Ah! That explains it, doesn't it? I was asleep and dreaming about fish. No problem. Open your mouth and say 'ahhhh.'"

"I already did."

"Well, do it again. I noticed something when you did it before." He opened his mouth, and I peered inside. "Has your tongue always been that long?"

"I yink yo."

"Don't talk with your mouth open. You need to have that tongue looked at."

"Hank, a pickup truck just pulled into the field, over there."

He pointed to a pickup that had come to a stop, an old faded green Chevy with a camper on the back.

"Drover, a strange pickup has just pulled into the field."

"Yeah, and it has four tires."

"Hmmm. Good point. It does have four tires. This is looking a little fishy to me."

"I thought we weren't going to talk about fish."

"What?"

"I didn't say anything."

"Good. Let's go!"

We shifted into Turbo Three and went streaking toward the unidentified pickup just as the driver stepped out. Description: a tall, skinny man with long, stringy hair hanging out of a battered straw cowboy hat, faded jeans, long-sleeved Western shirt with snap buttons, and a pair of dark eyes that seemed just a little bit shifty.

He was looking toward the hay truck, and he even leaned down so that he caught sight of Slim sleeping in the shade. I noticed that his eyebrows rose.

Right away, I had a bad feeling about this guy, so instead of doing the usual Hose Procedure on his tires, Drover and I slowed to a Stealthy Creep, raised the hair on our respective backs, and moved toward him. I wanted him to know right away that dogs were on duty and we would be watching his every move.

I figured he might jump back into the pickup when he saw us creeping toward him. People who don't belong on a ranch often do that, you know, and it's a sure sign that they're up to no good. But this guy flashed us a friendly smile, knelt down, and spoke to us.

"Hi, there. Come here."

We stopped in our tracks, leaving ten feet of space between us. I had no intention of getting too friendly too soon. I mean, when you're in the Security Business, you have to be suspicious of all strangers, no matter how nice they seem to be. It's pretty tough, being vigilant all the time, but it's something we have to do. Discipline is crucial.

The man smiled, as though he understood. "Well, that's okay. You dogs don't know who I am, so let me explain. My name's Willie Sidelow, and I'm with the Texas State Department of Hay. We need to make sure that all your equipment is up to standards, know what I mean?"

Oh. Well, that made sense. Sure.

He rose to his feet. "Now, I see that your master's taking himself a little nap and we don't need to disturb him. I'm going to send my assistant over to check out the truck, and then we'll be on our way." He turned toward the pickup. "Bub, come here!"

You won't believe this, but instead of opening the pickup door and stepping outside, Bub *jumped out the window*.

CHAPTER SIX

An Official Inspection

Pretty amazing, huh?

Bub was a little bitty feller, couldn't have stood more than three feet tall. He had big ears and you wouldn't describe his face as handsome, but other than that, he seemed fairly normal. He was dressed in jeans and a Western shirt, and had a red bandana around his neck and a black cowboy hat on his head.

He came over to Willie, who said, "Bub, these are the local guard dogs. Shake hands and let's be friends."

Bub stepped toward me and stuck out his hand. Okay, he wanted to shake hands, and I happened to be pretty good at that, so I offered a paw and we sealed our friendship with a shake.

Bub seemed a pretty swell guy, but when he offered his hand to Drover, the little mutt melted away and hid behind me.

"Drover, what are you doing? The man's trying to be neighborly. Shake his hand."

"Well . . . I don't know, there's something about him that makes me nervous."

"You're being weird, and you're embarrassing me. These guys are important officials. Shake his hand."

Wouldn't you know it? He cowered behind me and wouldn't come out to greet our guests.

But Willie was a good sport about it. He laughed and said, "That's okay. He's just a little bashful." He turned to his partner. "Okay, Bub, go check out the truck and we'll move on down the road."

Bub answered his boss with a snappy salute and headed for the truck. The little guy had plenty of energy. I mean, he didn't just *walk* to the truck. He ran. Anybody could see that he really enjoyed his work.

But then I noticed something kind of strange. After running upright for a ways, he dropped down on all fours and really scooted along. Gee, I didn't know many people who could run on all fours. And did I mention that he wasn't wearing shoes? No shoes.

Willie was watching me and said, "Bub got wounded in the war and sometimes he has to go down on his all fours. He'll never tell you this, but he won a cigar box full of medals in the Foreign Legion. He served two years in Abrakadabra. The man's a genuine hero, but you'd never know it, he's so quiet and humble." A quiver came into his voice, and he turned away. "It just breaks my heart to see him so crippled up."

I whirled around to Drover. "Did you hear that? Bub's a war hero, and you wouldn't even shake hands with him!"

"Well, he didn't look right."

"Drover, how would *you* look if you'd gone through years of fierce fighting? It takes a toll."

"Yeah, but . . ."

"I'm shocked, Drover. Shocked and very disappointed. I never dreamed that you could be so heartless and cruel."

I turned my back on him and . . . huh? Did you see that? Maybe not, because you weren't there, but I turned around just in time to see Bub jump through the window of the hay truck. I mean, one second he was sitting on the ground, and the next he was flying through the window.

For a guy who'd been crippled up in the war,

old Bub was a pretty good jumper.

Willie was watching me while he cleaned his fingernails with a pocketknife. "You know, there ain't many men who could do that, or who'd be brave enough to try. I mean, I've seen Bub's legs, and you wouldn't believe all the scars! Sword wounds and holes left by cannonballs, it almost makes you cry. What drives that little man is pure heart. I've never known a man who tried so hard. And I guess you've heard about his wife."

Uh . . . no.

"Sweetest little lady you ever met, a perfect saint, but she fell off a ladder and injured her back."

Gosh. Really?

"Hasn't known a day without pain since she was six years old, but she always has a smile and a kind word."

Bub came flying out the truck window, and he seemed to be carrying something in his hands.

Willie continued. "I think that's one thing that keeps Bub going, that smile on her lips and the glow of light in her face." He turned his gaze toward the sky. "Boys, sometimes I wish I could be half the man that Bub is. He's a real inspiration."

I turned to Drover. "Are you listening?"

His head was drooped and he began to sniffle.

"Yeah, and I don't think I can stand any more. I feel awful. It makes me want to crawl under my gunnysack and hide."

"When we get back to the office, you will stand with your nose in the corner for thirty minutes. And, Drover, I want you to think about what a rotten little mutt you've turned out to be."

"I will!" he moaned. "I can hardly stand myself, but I don't know where else to go."

Just then, Bub returned, and handed several items to Willie. Hmmm. That was odd. He had brought Slim's sack lunch, two hay hooks, and a box of socket wrenches from the truck. Willie looked them over and turned to me.

"We'll have to take this stuff back to the lab and run some tests." He pulled a sandwich out of the sack, looked it over, and smelled it. He made an awful face. "He eats this stuff?"

Right, yes. It was one of Slim's mackerel-and-ketchup sandwiches. He ate 'em all the time.

He offered the sandwich to Bub. Bub sniffed it, backed away, and shook his head, so Willie pointed it at me. "Y'all want this?"

Well, to be honest, I'd never shared Slim's fondness for canned mackerel (he ate it because it was cheap, don't you see), but what the heck, there was no sense in wasting a sandwich.

Willie pitched it in my direction, and I snatched it right out of the air. Three bites, one big gulp, and that sandwich was history. Too bad for Slim, heh heh, but maybe this would teach him not to sleep on the job.

Willie gave me and Drover a pat on the head. "What a couple of fine dogs, and smart? My lands, I don't recall ever meeting two smarter dogs. Well, we need to take these tools to the lab. When we get the results, we'll bring 'em right back, hear? Bye now."

Willie waved good-bye and so did Bub. They loaded up in the pickup and drove away. As I watched them drive out of sight, I heaved a sigh. "Gee, what a couple of great guys! You know, when you meet people like that, it kind of makes the world seem a little brighter, doesn't it?"

Drover didn't hear me. He had collapsed on the ground and was crying his heart out.

I stood over the runt for a minute, wondering what I should do. On the one hand, he didn't deserve any sympathy, after being so rude to our guests, but on the other hand . . . I really didn't want to listen to him bawl and squall for the rest of the day.

I gave him a pat on the shoulder. "Drover, I'm sure you didn't intend to be heartless and cruel."

"I really didn't," he blubbered, "but when Bub first walked up, I thought he looked like . . ."

"Like what? Go on, son, get it out of your system."

"You won't laugh at me?"

"Of course not. Who could laugh at a time like this?"

"Well, okay." He blinked back his tears and sat up. "He had hair on the back of his hand."

"No kidding? I didn't notice that."

"Yeah, and his mouth was too wide."

"Was it?"

"Yeah, and his ears were huge."

"They were big ears, weren't they?"

"Yeah, and when I looked at him, there for a second I thought he was . . . a monkey."

I stared at him. "A monkey? You thought Bub was a monkey?" I turned away and tried to hold back my laughter, but it all came spilling out. "Ha ha ha! You thought . . . ha ha ha!"

"You promised you wouldn't laugh."

"I know, but ha ha that's the funniest thing I ever heard! Ha ha! Bub is a famous war hero, but you thought . . . ha ha ha!"

Drover flopped back on the ground and started bawling again. "I'm never going to tell you any more secrets! All you ever do is laugh and make fun of me!"

At last I got control of myself and returned to his potsrate body. "All right, I'm sorry. I shouldn't have laughed, but honestly, Drover, sometimes you come up with the nuttiest ideas. I mean, those guys work for the State of Texas."

"How do you know that?"

"Because . . . well, because they said so."

"How do you know they weren't lying?"

"Drover, I can spot a liar a mile away. It's part of my training, and I'm seldom fooled."

"Yeah, but . . ."

"Hush and listen. I think I can clear this up right away." I began pacing in front of him, as I often do when I'm trying to pull heavy thoughts out of the vapors. "A monkey is a jungle animal, right? Is this a jungle?"

"No."

"Very good. A monkey walks around naked. Was he walking around naked as a jaybird?"

"I guess not."

"Don't guess, Drover, give me a straight answer. Was he naked or not?"

"No."

"Exactly. He was not naked. He was wearing cowboy clothes. It's common knowledge that monkeys never wear cowboy clothes."

"How come?"

"Because they're jungle animals. If a monkey wore clothes, he would wear a safari suit."

"Safari, so good."

"Exactly." I stopped pacing and whirled around. "And there we are. Through science and logic, we have disposed of your ridiculous Theory of Monkeys. Don't you feel better now?"

Drover was still scowling. "I'm not sure how I feel. You ate that whole sandwich and didn't even give me a bite."

"It wasn't that great, believe me . . . burp . . . excuse me, and don't try to change the subject. Everybody makes mistakes. Just admit that you were wrong."

He heaved a sigh. "Well, okay. You were wrong."

"Great. Thank you. Now we can . . ." Just then, I heard the sound of a vehicle approaching. I turned and saw a pickup pulling into the hay field. "There, you see? They've already finished their lab work. Those guys are really fast. And you thought they were just a couple of monkeys! Ha."

"I never said Willie was a monkey."

"Drover, just give it up."

I trotted toward the pickup just as Willie opened the door and stepped . . . HUH? I came to

62

a sudden stop. That wasn't Willie. It wasn't even a man. Unless my eyes were deceiving me...

CHAPTER SEVEN

My Beloved Comes Calling

"**H**oly smokes, Drover, it's Miss Viola!"

Drover's mouth dropped open. "Oh my gosh, it is! And you know what? I think she loves me!"

I couldn't believe it. The runt went streaking to Miss Viola, even though he knew perfectly well that I was her favorite dog in the whole world. I raced after him. "Drover, halt! Come back here! She's mine!"

Drover got there first and launched himself at her like . . . I don't know what, but it was a shocking and disgraceful display of Bad Dog Behavior. I mean, the ladies don't appreciate being mauled and pawed and slobbered on by dogs that have no manners.

I was so embarrassed by Drover's shabby behavior that I launched myself even higher in the air, flew right over the top of him, and landed right where I belonged—in the awaiting arms of the lady who adored me.

Okay, maybe I came on a little too strong and sent her staggering backwards, and maybe she uttered a sound that was somewhere between a squeak and a laugh, but by George when I got there, she knew I was glad to see her.

Remember Miss Viola? She lived down the creek with her aging parents and there were rumors that she was sweet on Slim, but my heart told a different story. When she came around, it was to see ME, not Slim, and certainly not Drover. And even though I almost knocked her down with love and adoration, I knew that she would understand.

Laughing, she stumbled backwards against the pickup. "Here, here, get down! I'm glad to see you, but I don't want to get mugged."

I turned a hot glare on Drover. "See what you've done? Shame on you! That's no way to treat a lady."

"Well, I was just . . ."

"Drover, sit down and behave yourself!" I turned my adoring gaze back on Miss Viola and was disappointed to see that she was looking toward the truck.

"Where's Slim?"

Who? Oh, him. Who cared about Slim, and could we change the subject? Back to ME, for example?

She started walking toward the truck. Drover and I had a little shoving match to see which of us got to walk beside her, and I won. This was great, a loyal dog and his lady fair, walking through the forest and sharing a few precious moments together.

Okay, it was a hay field, not a forest, but was I going to complain? No sir.

When we were about fifty feet from the truck, Viola saw Slim's boots sticking out from underneath. "Oh, there he is. Slim? Yoo-hoo? It's me, Viola. Slim? Slim!" When he didn't respond, a cloud of concern moved across her face. "Heavenly days, I hope he hasn't had a heart attack!"

A heart attack? Ha! He'd had a *sleep* attack, and I was just the dog who could cure him of that. I darted under the truck and licked his ear about ten times, until his eyes popped open and he gave me a shove backwards.

"Get away and quit licking my dadgum ear!" He crawled out from under the truck, grumbling and muttering. "A man can't even grab a decent nap around here without . . ." He saw Viola and froze. "Good honk. Viola!"

She heaved a sigh and looked up at the sky. "Slim Chance, you scared the daylights out of me! I thought you'd had a heart attack!"

He stood up and gave her a grin. "No, I had a sinking spell, is all, and felt a powerful need for a nap."

She laughed. "Well, I'm sure glad. I was just trying to figure out how I'd get you to the hospital."

"How would you have done it?"

"Well, I knew I couldn't load you in the back of the pickup, so I'd about decided to throw Daddy's log chain around your ankles and drag you."

He got a big laugh out of that. "I'd have been pretty skinned up by the time we got to town. I'm glad you checked first." He shuffled his feet and stared at the ground. "Viola, it's kind of embarrassing to get caught sleeping in the middle of the day."

"Why? Daddy takes a nap every day."

"Yeah, but he's a hundred years old. I like to think that I'm still a bronking buck."

"Oh, fiddle. Don't worry about it." Her smile faded. "Slim, Daddy sent me up here to see if you-all were missing any tools. He went to the shop this morning and couldn't find his impact wrench, and there were several other things missing."

Slim leaned against the truck. "Nope, I haven't noticed anything."

"Well, maybe he was mistaken. He's forgetful sometimes." She glanced around. "Are you hauling this hay by yourself?"

"Yep, just me and the dogs. Loper and Sally May took off on a little vacation to the mountains."

"Well"—she shrugged her shoulders and smiled—"I guess I'd better drive the truck for you."

His eyes popped open. "Would you mind? Boy, that would make it go twice as fast. And heck, we could even say that we're having a date."

She stared at him for a moment. "Slim, I'll be glad to help you, but this is *not* a date. Nobody goes on a date in a hay field. They go to a movie or a restaurant or a country dance."

"Oh." Slim hitched up his jeans. "Well, I thought we might double up and save some time."

"No. One of these days we'll get dressed up and go somewhere nice, and *that* will be a date."

"Sure seems like a lot of trouble."

"Slim Chance, honestly! You'd better quit talking before you lose your truck driver."

Slim ducked his head as though she'd chunked a rock at him, and opened the door of the truck. "Let me get my hooks." He rummaged around inside the cab. "Well, that's crazy. I can't find my derned hay hooks, and I know I left 'em in here. And my socket set. And my lunch!" He crawled out of the cab and looked her in the eyes. "Viola, there's something strange going on around here."

As you might expect, I had been listening to their conversation, and I thought it was pretty funny. I gave Drover an elbow in the ribs.

"Hey, Drover, did you hear that? Slim thinks somebody swiped his hay hooks!"

"Yeah, 'cause somebody did."

"No, no, you've missed the point. See, he slept through the visit of the guys from the State Department of Hay. He doesn't understand that they took his stuff to the lab for some testing. Ha ha."

"Oh. Yeah. Testing. Tee hee. That's pretty funny."

"It's a scream. Look at those dark lines on his face. Why, he thinks he's been burglarized."

"Yeah, tee hee. Maybe we ought to tell him what happened."

I gave that some thought. "You know, we should, but how do you say 'Texas Department of Hay' in Tailwag?"

"Well, let me think here. Two wags up and down, and three sideways?"

"No, that means 'good morning.'"

"Oh, yeah. Well, how about three wags up and down, and four sideways?"

I curled my lip at him. "Drover, have you forgotten everything? That means 'Where's the food?'"

"Well, everything's different when you've got a stub tail."

"No, it's all the same, only your messages are shorter and mine are longer, but never mind because I don't know how to say it either."

I turned back to Slim and listened. He was staring off in the distance and seemed to be deep in thought. He raised a finger in the air. "Wait a second. A deputy sheriff stopped by yesterday and said . . . hmmm, I wonder . . ."

He dropped his gaze to the ground and started walking, looking for tracks. Again, I nudged Drover. "He's going to find Bub's tracks, but he'll never figure it out."

"Yeah, I wish we could tell him the whole story."

"Me too, but sometimes the communication barriers are just too great."

Slim stopped and knelt down. His finger drew a circle in the dust. His head came up and he turned to Viola. "I just figured it out. These are *monkey tracks*."

HUH?

My gaze slid sideways until I found myself staring into Drover's eyes. "Did you hear what I just heard?"

"Yeah. Monkey tracks."

"Right. Do you remember the discussion we had about Bub, about how he looked odd?"

"Yeah, and I said he looked like a monkey."

"No, I said that. I mean, I noticed his ears right away, and . . . well, he wasn't wearing boots, and right then I started getting suspicious, very suspicious, and I believe I said, 'Drover, that guy looks like a monkey dressed up in cowboy clothes.' I'm almost sure . . ."

Slim's voice boomed, "Hank!"

"Drover, I think it's time for us to disappear."

"I hear that."

Without being too obvious about our intentions, we, uh, slithered across an empty space of ground and took refuge beneath the truck. There, we waited and listened to the pounding of our respective hearts. Some inner instinct told me that . . . well, we might be in trouble.

But Slim would never think to look for us

under the truck. Would he?

I couldn't see all of him, just the lower part of his body from the waist down, and I'm sorry to report that the lower portion of his body seemed to be moving . . . gulp . . . in our direction, and I had every reason to suppose that his upper body was coming along with the lower portion. His legs and boots walked to the edge of the truck bed and stopped.

Then his head appeared. He crooked his index finger, as if to say, "Come here."

I turned to Drover. "He's calling you."

"Me? I thought it was for you."

"No, he's giving you a summons to report to the front immediately.'"

"Oh, darn. What does he want?"

"At this point, we don't know for sure, but I would guess that . . . well, he wants to ask you a question or two."

"Yeah, but I don't know any answers."

"Drover, just give him a blank stare, the usual stuff. Go on."

He didn't go cheerfully, but he went, mainly because I gave him a shove. He groveled over to Slim. Slim shook his head. "Uh uh." He pointed a skinny finger at . . . well, at ME, it appeared, and growled, "You. Bozo. Come here."

Drover and I
Figure It Out

I grabbed a deep breath of air and began crawling toward him, rehearsing my story as I went. This wasn't going to be fun. I crawled out into the sunlight and gave him a grin that said:

"Okay, those tracks. We noticed them too, but we have no idea where they came from. We were wondering if they might be . . . well, fossilized monkey tracks. You know, tracks that have been here for thousands and thousands of years. See, once upon a time, when the world was young, bands of wild monkeys roamed across the ranch and . . ."

I studied his face, and right away I knew that he wasn't buying my story. Gulp. Then he spoke. "Hank, what happened while I was asleep?"

I felt myself wilting under the heat of his gaze. It was . . . it was hard to explain . . . impossible to explain, actually. I mean, it was beginning to appear that Willie and Bub might have been impostors.

Are you shocked? So was I. They had told us an incredible pack of lies, and we'd been completely hoodwinked.

My head sank, and I felt rotten.

Slim turned to Viola and told her about Deputy Kile's report on the Monkey Gang. She was astonished. "He uses a monkey to steal? And you think they robbed Daddy's shop? Slim, this is really bizarre! But how did the monkey get past Daddy's dogs? Blackie and Jackie hear everything."

"Well, the deputy said they give goofy pills to the dogs." He glared down at me. "But I guess they decided my dogs were goofy enough and didn't need any pills. They watched the whole thing and didn't even raise a squeak." His eyes widened. "Say, we'd better jump in your pickup and check things up at headquarters. Those crooks might still be around. Come on!"

They got into Viola's pickup and roared away, leaving Drover and me sitting in the glare of our own failure.

"Drover, how could we have allowed this to

happen? What went wrong?"

"I don't know. I guess it was the clothes that fooled us."

"You're right. Who would ever expect to see a monkey wearing a cowboy costume?"

"Not me. It's not fair—they cheated."

"They really did. They thought they could make chumps out of us, dressing the monkey in clothes. And you know what? It worked. We were chumps, Drover. We fell for the whole shabby mess."

"Yeah, and I feel awful about it."

I began pacing back and forth in front of him. "But we can't just roll over and die. We must learn from our bitter experience and come back again: stronger, wiser, and tougher dogs."

He stared at me through his tears. "What do you mean?"

I whirled around and faced him. "I mean if the Monkey Gang strikes again, we'll be ready for them."

"We will?"

"Yes sir. We won't be fooled by the phony cowboy clothes, and next time when we see a midget with monkey ears and a monkey mouth, we'll know that he's a monkey."

"Gosh, I never thought of that. But what if

they try to give us goofy pills?"

"We'll laugh in their faces and put 'em under arrest!" I began pacing again as my mind raced toward huge thoughts and concepts. "Never again, Drover. Until we break this case, all leaves are cancelled. We'll work twenty-four hours a day straight through, no breaks, no sleep, no rest, no food."

His eyes popped open. "No food?"

"That's correct. We stop for nothing or no one. Until we get those creeps behind bars, we will be oblidious to pain and the needs of the body. Oblibious. Ablibious. What is the word I'm searching for?"

"Well, let me think here. 'Ham bone'?"

"No."

He wadded up his mouth. "Uh . . . 'bacon'?"

"No, a big word. Think, Drover."

"'Elephant'?"

"Wait, I've got it. 'Oblivious.'"

"Never heard of it."

"Until we wrap up this case, we will be oblidious to all the so-forth." Viola's pickup was coming back toward the hay field. "Well, they didn't find the crooks. Quick, under the truck. Maybe Slim will forget we're here."

We scooted ourselves under the hay truck and

became invisible to human eyes and enemy radar. The pickup stopped and two doors slammed. Slim and Viola made their way toward the truck, and I could hear them talking.

Slim: "Well, they missed a good chance there, but they're liable to come back after dark. If they do, I'll be ready for 'em."

Viola: "Slim, please, just call the sheriff."

"I ain't calling the sheriff."

"Why?"

"Viola, when you call the sheriff, it ends up in the local newspaper. I can see it now: 'While Slim Chance, local cowboy hero, was taking his afternoon nap under the hay truck, two hay hooks and a socket set disappeared from the cab. Mr. Chance couldn't describe the suspects, didn't write down the license plate number, and never even saw a vehicle, but he did find a monkey track in the dirt.'"

"I see what you mean."

"I'd be laughed out of the county. If Loper read that in the paper, he'd holler and squall for three days. I'd never hear the end of it."

"Well, promise that you won't do anything foolish."

"I never set out to do anything foolish. It just turns out that way sometimes."

"Slim! Promise."

"Okay, I promise that I won't shoot out his headlights, radiator, and all four tires. I won't take a piece of windmill rod and whip him and his frazzling monkey all the way up to Kansas, although that might be fun."

"Nothing dangerous or foolish?"

"All I want is a tag number and a description of the pickup. Then I'll call the sheriff, and there won't be any mention of me taking a nap."

"Fair enough. Well, you said something about hauling hay?"

"It ain't moved. You still offering to drive?"

"Let the adventure begin."

"Heh. Well, driving that old truck will give you plenty of adventure."

At this point, you're probably worried sick that Drover and I got squashed under the wheels of the hay truck, right? I mean, we'd found it convenient to vanish for a while, and we'd gone into Stealthy Silence under the truck, so you might say that our lives were in serious danger.

Actually, the danger factor was pretty small. A dog would have to be deaf and blind to get squashed under that particular truck, and do you know why? Because when they fired up the motor, it made such an awful roar and sent out such a

cloud of smoke, even a rock would have moved.

We moved, with time to spare, and spent the rest of the day on rodent duty in the hay field. By this time, Slim had other things on his mind besides the Monkey Episode, such as blistered fingers, aching muscles, stickers in his elbows, dehydration, and sweat-burned eyes, and it all added up to a pleasant afternoon. When Slim is bone-tired and dripping sweat, he's pretty easy to get along with.

It must have been around eight o'clock that evening when we backed the last load of hay into the stack lot. Slim mopped his face with a bandana and pulled off his leather gloves. "I'll stack it tomorrow," he said to Viola. "I'm beat and I know you are too, riding in that hot truck all afternoon." He sat down on the running board and caught his breath. "I sure appreciate your help, Viola. Would you let me pay you something?"

She gave him an odd smile. "Yes, but not money."

"Uh-oh. What have I got myself into?"

She looked off into the distance. "Frankie McWhorter is playing a dance at Lipscomb tomorrow night."

Slim flinched and stared at the ground. "Well, I'm too tired to argue. I guess if you're brave enough to dance with me, I'm brave enough take you." With much grunting and grumbling, he jacked himself up to a standing position. "I'll walk you to your pickup."

She placed her hand in the crook of his arm, and they headed for her pickup. "You look exhausted. How are you going to stay awake tonight?"

"I don't plan to stay awake."

"What about the thieves?"

"Oh, yeah, I almost forgot. Well, I don't know, but I'll manage somehow. I already know I can't depend on them dogs. I'd get more help out of a couple of cinder blocks."

What? Did you hear that? Why, I'd never been so insulted. Hey, just because we'd messed up the first time didn't mean we would let it happen again. For his information, I was wide-awake and loaded for bear. And mad too. If that monkey showed up on my ranch again, he was going to get a rude surprise.

Slim walked her to the pickup and opened the door. They stood there for a moment, as though neither knew what to say. Viola fussed with a button on her blouse, while Slim rocked up and down on his toes and jingled some coins in his pocket. Then he cut his eyes from side to side, grabbed a big gulp of air, bent down, and gave her a peck on the cheek.

"Thanks again. See you tomorrow evening." He hurried away.

She smiled, touched the spot he had kissed, and drove off.

I turned to Drover. "Did you see that?"

His face melted into a grin. "Yeah, how sweet!"

"Sweet, my foot. He has his nerve, planting kisses on my lady friend."

"Are you jealous?"

"What do you think? Of course I'm jealous. She came over here to see ME. I turn my back on him for a minute, and he's kissing her on the cheek!"

"Well, I think maybe she came to see him, not you."

"Drover, anyone can see that she's nuts about me. Why, I'm surprised she didn't slap him baldheaded. And if he ever does that again, I hope she does."

"She won't."

"What?"

"I said, I'm starved."

At that very moment, my stomach growled. "Yes, I'm kind of hungry myself. Let's grab some supper. This could be a long night."

We made our way up to the machine shed, where we found the overturned Ford hubcap that served as our dog bowl. Slim had filled it to the brim with kernels of Co-op dog food, and we hacked our way through about half of it.

Was it delicious? No, but it would keep us alive until something better came along. That's the best you can say about Co-op dog food.

We Prepare
for the Worst

A round dark, Slim finished his chores at the corrals and joined us in front of the machine shed. Dragging himself along like an old man, he sat down on an overturned bucket in front of the shed and stared at the ground with glazed eyes.

"Dogs, here's the plan. We've got to stay up tonight and keep a watch. The trouble is, I'm wore out and hungry, and I smell like a billy goat."

Hmm. Good point. I hadn't wanted to say anything, but, yes, he did smell a little ripe, after sweating all day in the field.

"I'm going to raid Sally May's icebox and fix myself a bite of supper. Then I'm going to crawl into her bathtub and soak for about half an hour." He slapped his hands on his knees and pushed himself up. "Maybe a nice hot bath will wake me

85

up."

What? He thought that soaking in a tub of hot water would *wake him up*?

Maybe I should have barked a protest and tried to argue the point, but I had no reason to suppose that he would listen to me. They never do, you know. One of the first things a cowdog learns about his job is that his people really don't want to know what he thinks.

It's too bad. We dogs could spare them a lot of grief if they would just listen to us, but they don't and there's nothing we can do about it.

He took a big yawn and stretch, then his eyes drifted down to me. The lines in his brow hardened. "Hank, I don't know what kind of foolishness went on between you and that monkey this afternoon, but if he shows up again tonight, I'd sure appreciate it if you'd remember who buys your dog food." He leaned down into my face. "It ain't a monkey. Am I making myself clear?"

Well, sure . . . yes. Of course.

"If you want to be pals with a monkey, do it on your own time."

I did NOT want to be pals with a monkey, and there was no need for Slim to rub salsa into old wounds.

He turned and started toward the house. "You

act like a monkey about half the time, but try to remember that you're a dog."

Oh, brother. Make one little mistake around here and they throw it on you like a saddle and ride you until you drop. For his information, I had spent the entire afternoon roasting over the fires of guilt, and had concluded on my own that . . . yes, Drover had made a serious mistake and had failed his ranch. And I had no intention of letting it happen again.

Slim shuffled down to the house and disappeared inside. As darkness fell around me, I realized that . . . yawn . . . gee, I was really bushed. I mean, chasing rodents all day in the hot sun . . . yawn . . . will suck the life right out of a . . . yawn . . . dog.

And all at once, I began to . . . yawn . . . wonder if I could . . .

I know what you're thinking. You think I rushed down to the gas tanks, fell into the loving embrace of my gunnysack bed, and didn't move a hair until morning. And while I slept, the Monkey Burglars came and stole half the ranch.

Isn't that exactly what you were thinking? Go ahead and admit it.

Well, I have two words to say to that: ha ha. That's the most ridiculous, the most outrageous

. . . okay, maybe it's not so ridiculous, and just to prove what kind of dog I am, I'm going to admit, here and now, in front of everybody, that I was tempted to sprint down to the gas tanks and dive into the awaiting arms of my gunnysack bed.

But get this: I didn't do it. I imposed Higher Discipline upon myself and stayed awake, so you were wrong. Are you sorry that you doubted me? You should be.

I stayed awake, even though I could hear my gunnysack singing a lullaby and calling my name. Then, sometime in the deep dark of night, I saw a pair of headlights creeping toward ranch headquarters, and heard the sound of an unidentified vehicle.

Okay, let's be honest. Drover was the first to turn in the report. "Hank, wake up! Somebody's here. Hank?"

I leaped to my feet. "Everybody stand back, don't panic. Drover, is that you?"

"Where?"

"There, right in front of your stub tail."

He looked at his tail. "Yeah, it's me."

"Good, I thought so." I blinked my eyes. "Drover, I have a feeling that something's going on around here."

"Yeah, something is. A pickup just stopped at

the mailbox."

"A pickup!" I swung my gaze around to the north, just in time to see a pair of headlights go dark. A chill of dread cut a path down the middle of my back. "Holy smokes, they're back! Where is Slim?"

"I don't know. He went down to the house three hours ago and never came back."

"What!"

"Hank, what are we going to do? What if it's that monkey again?"

By this time, the vaporous waves of vapor had . . . okay, maybe I had slipped into a very light doze, but now I was back on the job

"Drover, listen carefully. We don't have much time. I'm going to rush down to the house and bark the alarm. I don't know what Slim's doing in there, but we need him out here right away. While I'm gone, you go up to the machine shed and stand guard. Got it?"

"Got it."

"Be a brave little soldier, and I'll see you on the other side."

In the privacy of my mind, I strapped on the tanks of my Rocket Dog suit, turned the controls to Turbo Five, and went roaring down to the house, followed by a long streak of yellow flames and smoke. At the yard gate, I screeched to a halt and unbuckled the RD equipment. I was about to sound the alarm when I noticed . . .

"Drover? I thought you were guarding the machine shed. That was our plan."

"Yeah, but I thought of a better plan: Stay close to you."

"Why?"

"Well . . . I'm kind of scared of monkeys."

"Oh, brother. Okay, it's too late to spill the milk. Let's go into Code Three Barking. Ready? Hit it!"

Boy, you should have heard us. We leaned into those Code Threes and really rattled the windows. Very impressive barking. Then we waited for Slim to come bursting out the door. Seconds passed, minutes. Nothing.

"What is wrong with that guy! How can I protect this ranch if he . . . wait a second, I just figured it out. He fell asleep in the bathtub! I knew it, I tried to tell him. Okay, son, I'm going into the yard, and I may have to tear down the door to dig him out of there. You wait here and keep a lookout. Got it?"

"Got it."

"If a monkey tries to offer you some pills, don't take 'em."

"Got it."

"Good luck, soldier."

I coiled up the enormous muscles in my hind legs and went flying over the fence. Back on Planet Earth, I sprinted toward a window on the north side of the house, which I happened to know was the bathroom window. There, I spread out all four legs, went into the Barking Stance, and prepared to . . .

"Drover? What are you doing here? You're supposed to be standing guard at the gate."

"Yeah, but . . ." He keeled over, kicked all four legs, and started bawling. "I'm so scared, I don't know what I'm doing!"

I glared down at him for a moment, shaking my head and wondering how one little mutt could be so worthless. "Okay, never mind. I've got to stick with the plan."

"I feel awful about this!"

I stepped over his carcass and hopped up on the side of the house, until I could see through the window. I knew it! There he was, stretched out in the tub with water up to his chin and a peaceful grin on his face.

Well, you know me. When Duty calls, I get pretty serious about things. I barked and I barked and I barked—big barks, manly barks, the kind of barks that can cause a rock to jump up and start

dancing.

Again, I peered through the window . . . and couldn't believe my eyes. He was still asleep and hadn't even moved! And at that very moment I heard a sound up at the machine shed. I cocked my ear and listened: a rattle, a clink. *Someone was inside the machine shed!*

I cut my eyes from side to side. My mind was swirling. What should I do? Drover had gone into a swoon, and Slim was asleep in the bathtub. Should I stay at the house, claw the screen off the window, dive through the window glass, and make a desperate attempt to get Slim's attention?

Or should I march up to the machine shed and take care of the nasty business without any backup?

Time was slipping away, and my heart was pounding like the beat of a heartbeat. I had to do something. I decided to take matters into my own hands. If I went down in battle, at least I would go out protecting my ranch. I would be honored and mourned. Sally May would cry when she got the news, and Miss Viola would throw herself across the casket and weep for days, crushed by the loss of her beloved Hank.

When she learned that Slim had slept through the tragedy, she would refuse to go dancing with him, and maybe even refuse to speak to him again, and the cause of Justice would be served.

I took a big gulp of air, perhaps one of my last, whirled around, and began my fateful march to the machine shed. But first I tripped over Drover. "Idiot! If you can't help, at least get out of the way."

"Help!"

"Our machine shed is being robbed."

"Hank, this leg's killing me!"

"I don't care. While I'm gone, maybe you could bark a few times and try to get Slim out of the bathtub."

"I'll try. Oh, the guilt!"

I left him there and marched across the yard to the fence. My newly discovered reserves of courage lasted, oh, maybe five steps. At that point, I stopped and realized that . . . gulp . . . I was going into this action all alone and without backup. I would be going up against a professional monkey burglar, and I had no idea what kind of resistance he might offer.

I mean, the guy had been trained to rob, so maybe he'd been trained to fight too: boxing, wrestling, karate, kajudo. Did he carry a billy club? A sword? I looked back toward the house. The light from the window spilled out into the yard, revealing that Drover was sitting up.

"Uh . . . Drover, you're looking better now. Listen, pal, I was wondering if you might . . ."

BAM. He was stretched out again. "Oh, darn, there for a second the pain went away, but then it came back, and now it's worse than ever! You'd better go on without me."

Great.

CHAPTER TEN

The Moment of Truth Draws Near

Have you ever noticed that Drover's leg attacks seem to come at the very times when I could use his help the most? I've noticed it. There seems to be a pattern, and it's caused me to wonder . . . oh well. The point is that I could scratch him off the list of possible backups.

I leaped over the fence and began my fateful march up the hill to the machine shed. Again, I heard clinks and clanks, rattles and rumbles, coming from inside. This did very little to build up my reserves of courage. In fact . . .

HUH?

At that very moment, when my reserves of courage had just about hit bottom, I looked up and saw . . . yipes! A shadowy form was sprinting down the hill, coming directly at me! Holy smokes, the monkey had decided to attack me before I could attack him!

The hair on my back stood straight up—I mean, we're talking about a Mohawk haircut all the way from my ears to the base of my tail. I screeched to a stop and was about to haul the mail back to the house, when I noticed . . .

Wait! It was only a cat. Pete. Ha ha. Did that give you a little scare? It did me.

"Pssst. Pete, over here." When kitty heard my voice, he slowed to a walk and crept toward me. He was glancing around with big eyes. "Hey, Pete, it's really great to see you again, no kidding."

"Hankie, you might want to know that someone's in the machine shed."

"Right. I knew that, Pete, and I was on my way to . . . uh . . . check it out. Listen, pal, I've been thinking. It bothers me that you and I never . . . well, do anything together."

"Oh, really?"

"Right. Sometimes it seems that all we ever do is fight and argue. And, Pete, that's not good. I mean, we live on the same ranch, share the same air and sunshine . . ."

His big yellow eyes seemed to glow in the light of the moon. "What's the point, Hankie?"

"The point? Ha ha. Pete, I don't have any point. Okay, maybe a small point." I laid a paw on his shoulder. "Pete, how would you like to go to work for the Security Division? We've never hired a cat before, but I've been watching you and . . . Pete, I'm impressed. Honest."

"Let me guess, Hankie. You want me to go with you to the machine shed?"

I gave him an astonished look. "I hadn't thought of that, Pete, but you know, it's a pretty good idea. No, it's a great idea. I mean, we could put you right to work, get you on the payroll and everything. And I think you'd enjoy the challenge, I really do."

"What does it pay?"

"Pay? Ha ha. Well, Pete, a lot of our compensation comes from the satisfaction of doing a good job, know what I mean?"

He pulled away from me. "That's what I thought, Hankie. I think I'll pass."

"What? Wait a second, don't leave." My mind was racing. "Okay, Pete, let's cut the chatter and go straight to the bottom line. I've never asked a favor of you, but tonight, Pete, I need your help."

"I'm sure you do."

"So I guess I'm putting our friendship on the line. What do you say?"

"No."

"You don't have to give me an answer right this minute."

He walked away. "No."

I followed him. "I'm sure you'll want to think it over."

"No."

"There's no big rush."

"No."

I dived in front of him and glared into his cunning little eyes. "What do you mean, no?"

He heaved a sigh. "Hankie, I don't know who that is in the machine shed, but he doesn't belong on this ranch."

"I'm aware of that, kitty, and that's why I need your help. Would you want me to go in there all alone? Without a backup or even a companion to give me moral support?"

He tapped his paw on the ground for a moment. "Yes, I think that would be all right."

"What!"

He sprinted off into the darkness. "Good luck, Hankie."

"Come back here, you little weasel! Pete!"

He was gone, and I was alone again.

Now you know why we never hire cats. When the chips are down, the cats are gone.

They're lazy, arrogant, selfish, cunning, and deceitful. Friendship means nothing to a cat. They'll love you and leave you, only they never loved you in the first place. A cat loves himself first, foremost, and forever, and the rest of the world can go to blazes.

I was right back where I'd started, only I'd made a fool of myself by offering the scheming little fraud a great career opportunity. I should have known better, and I was tickled pink that he'd turned me down.

No, I wasn't. I was scared silly, if you must know the truth, so scared that my legs felt like stalks of wilted celery. Could I go on with my lonely mission? Did I have the strength and courage to bust into the machine shed and engage a gangster monkey in hand-to-hand combat?

I looked up at the dark sky and took several deep breaths of air. Only the distant stars understood the loneliness of being at the top, because they were at the top of everything. But there was one difference between me and the stars. All they had to do was twinkle. I had to PERFORM. No amount of twinkling would get me off the hook if that little monkey hauled off all the ranch's tools.

Slim could sleep in the bathtub. Drover could

go on the sick list. Pete could be his usual slacker self. Me? I was Head of Ranch Security.

There was nothing left to say, nothing more to discuss. I turned my nose toward the west and began my lonely trudge up the hill. When I reached the gravel drive, I marched with long determined strides to the big sliding double doors. I was very tempted to stop and think about what I was getting myself into, but I knew that if I ever stopped, I might never summon the courage to finish the job.

I didn't slow down or miss a step. I took aim for the gap between the . . . HUH? There he stood: a midget with big ears and a wide mouth . . . . carrying an armload of tools. But here's the part that almost blew me away. You thought I'd find Bub, dressed up in his cowboy costume? Me too. That's exactly what I'd expected, but that's not what I saw.

I saw . . . A GIRL.

No kidding. A monkey girl! She was wearing a short pink dress, a white blouse with fringe on the sleeves, and she had long red hair. She wore lipstick on her mouth and circles of red paint on her cheeks. What do you call that stuff? Rouge. Yes, she had circles of rouge on her cheeks.

For a moment of heartbeats, we stared into

each other's eyes. She seemed as shocked to see me as I was to see her. Very shocked.

Well, what's a guy supposed to do when he catches a girl monkey stealing tools out of his barn? If this had been Bub in his cowboy outfit, I would have thrashed him on the spot—no questions, no prisoners, no deals, no mercy. But a girl?

It took me a moment to find my voice. "Okay, sweetheart, I'm with the Security Division. Drop the tools."

The tools crashed to the ground. I marched a circle around her, studying every clue and detail. She didn't move and seemed terrified. This was good. Maybe I could make the arrest without any great bloodshed.

"What's your name?"

In a tiny squeak of a voice, she said, "Lucy."

"I see. Well, Lucy, I'm sorry to tell you this, but you're in serious trouble."

"I know."

"You've been caught in the act of stealing tools from my ranch."

"I know."

I stopped in front of her. "You look pretty scared."

"I am."

"So . . . does this mean you've never done this sort of thing before?"

"No sir, never."

I paced around her again. "Just as I thought. I'm beginning to see a pattern here. Willie's the boss of your gang, and he works two monkeys. Bub works the day shift, am I right?" She nodded. "You're the new kid, and the boss is starting you out on the night shift, right?"

In a quivering voice, she said, "Yes sir."

"It's all very clever. You and Bub do the stealing and Willie sells the loot. Where does he sell the stuff, at auctions?"

"Yes sir, and pawnshops in Oklahoma."

"Just as I figured. Does he cut you in on the dough?"

"Well, sir"—her sad little eyes drifted to the ground—"he gives us two bananas a day."

"Two bananas. Gee, what a hero."

"And a box of Yum-Yums."

"What are Yum-Yums?"

"Candy. You want one?"

"No, thanks. I never eat candy on the job." I paced another circle around her, then stopped and looked her in the eyes. "Lucy, how did a nice girl like you get mixed up with a bum like Willie? I mean, for crying out loud, the guy's a crook!"

104

"I know. I just . . ." She covered her face with her hands and burst into tears. I waited for her to get control of herself, but she kept crying. This was making me uneasy, so I laid a paw on her shoulder and told her to sit down.

"There, there, don't cry. You're in big trouble, but it's not the end of the world."

She sat down on the cement pad in front of the barn doors, and gazed up at me with tear-shimmering eyes. "You seem very kind, sir."

"Actually, I'm not kind at all, Lucy. I'm pretty hard-boiled and rarely show any emotion in my work, but . . . well, there's something about your situation that touches me."

"You *are* kind, and I only wish . . ." She turned away.

"You wish what? Tell me."

"I only wish . . . that you'd accept a small gift of friendship. A Yum-Yum."

"Lucy, we're not supposed to accept gifts from strangers. It's one of our rules."

A look of hurt filled her eyes and her lip began to quiver. "Oh, sir, I'm not a stranger! I've known me all my life."

"Well, sure, but I mean . . ."

She clasped her hands in front of her. "I know I've been a bad girl, but if you think I'm

105

strange"—she started crying again—"it just breaks my heart!"

I moved a few inches away to avoid the splash of her tears. "Okay, Lucy, if it will make you feel better, I'll accept your gift."

CHAPTER ELEVEN

Lucy's
Heartrending Story

She stopped crying and reached into a pocket on the front of her dress. She pulled out a little box of candy. "Here, take them all."

"No, just one. Since you've got fingers, you dig it out of the box."

She opened the top of the box with her little monkey hands and offered me a roundish piece of chocolate candy. She laid it down on the cement, and I gave it a thorough sniffing.

I mean, Lucy seemed like a nice kid, but I didn't want to take any chances. When you're dealing with the crinimal element, you never know. Don't forget what Deputy Kile had said about the sleeping pills.

It passed my Snifferation Test. This was

chocolate candy, not some kind of goofball medicine. I swept it into my mouth and chewed it. My ears shot up. "Hey, this is the good kind, with mushamino cherries in the center. Wow, I love 'em!"

A grin spread across her mouth, and . . . you know, it just got wider and wider. Nobody ever said that monkeys have pretty mouths. They don't, not even the girls. "Would you like another?"

"No, thanks. One's plenty. Go on with your story. How in thunderation did you get mixed up with a gang of robbers?"

Her smile faded and she looked away. "I was a rebellious child."

"I thought so. We hear this a lot."

"I never listened to my mother. We fought all the time, and I ran away from home and . . . joined the circus."

"Lucy, Lucy! I've never met your mother, but you should have listened to her. Mothers always know best. A circus is no place for a gerp. A girl, that is."

"I know that now, but I was stubborn and headstrong. You want another Yum-Yum?"

"No, thanks." My tongue swept across my lips. "Sure, what the heck, one more."

She brought a piece of candy out of the box.

"Let me show you a trick we did in the circus." She pitched it up in the air. "Snap it."

I watched as the candy arced gracefully into the air. Then, when it had reached its peak and started to come down, I opened my mouth, shifted my head slightly, and snapped it right out of the air. "Hey, did you see that? Maybe I should have gotten a job in the circus, huh?"

"That was good, sir. You seem to be very talented."

I couldn't help chuckling. "Well, I'm not one to brag, Lucifer, but . . ."

"Lucy."

"Lucy. Sorry. I'm not one to bag, but yes, I'm fairly tounted. Anyway, go on with your story. You joined the curpus. Circus." I stared at her face and noticed something odd. "Luby, do you have three eyes?"

"Why, no sir, only two."

"Huh. That's fumble . . . uh, funny. There for a second, I thought I saw tree eyes."

She giggled. "Oh, sir, you're teasing me."

"I am?"

"Yes sir, because trees don't have eyes."

"Oh. Ha ha. You're right, but I said *three* eyes, not . . . does it seem cold out here?"

"No sir, maybe a little warm."

"That's what I meant. I'm burping up."

"You're sick?"

"No, I said I'm *burning up*. Hot. Maybe I nerd some air." I stood up and paced a few . . . now, that was really odd. My back legs just quit on me, and all at once I was . . . well, pulling myself along with my hiney dragging the ground.

She noticed this and squeaked a laugh. "Oh, sir, you do the funniest things! It's hard to believe that you're a mean old guard dog."

"Ha ha. Yes, well, anything to impress the ladies, I always say, but actually . . . Loopy, all at wump things seem to be spinning around. Are you noticing anything lipe that?"

She gazed up at the sky. "Well, sir, they say the earth is spinning around all the time. We just don't notice it."

"Yeah, well, sullenly I notice it." I dragged myself over to her. "Lizzie, I muss ask you a merry important quejon . . . question."

She sat up and gave me her full attention. "Yes, sir?"

I leaned toward her . . . actually, I fell into her lap. "Oops, sorry." I gathered myself up, swaying back and forth. "Lukie, tell me the troof, the honest troof. I mutts know. Bottom line: Are you a good lil mucky or a bad lil mucky?"

She gave me an odd smile. "The truth? You want the truth?" I happened to be looking directly at her when she . . . HUH? Peeled off the red wig and pitched it on the ground, and wiped the lipstick on the back of her hand. And when she spoke, her voice had changed. "Check it out. I'm Bub, same guy. Hee hee. Did I fool you?"

I tried to steady myself and beamed her . . . beamed *him* a gaze of purest steel. "Mot even for a mimute. I wasss on to your triss from very start, Bug."

His shoulders twitched in a shrug. "Oh, well. I knew I'd get caught sooner or later. I guess I'm under arrest, huh?"

"Thass right, pal. You're unner rest."

"I don't care. You know, I hate this job. It's so . . . so degrading, know what I mean?"

I put my nose in his face. "Then why dun you juss run away? Muckys who hate their jobs *quit*, pal."

He rolled his eyes up to the sky. "I never thought of it that way. Good point. There's the other side, isn't there? The food is pretty good and . . . well, it's interesting work, like being a movie star or something. You know, costumes, acting, adventure all the time." He let out a weird giggle. "Gosh, maybe I don't hate my job after all."

112

I tried to pull myself up to a dignified pose. "Thass juss what I thought, Blub. You shunt have come bakk eer. See, this issss smy ransh, and now I'm gun haff to arress you."

"Yes, you keep saying that, but . . ." He grinned and gave me a wink. "Are you sure you can stay awake?"

"Huh? Sssure I kin say wake."

"I wonder. Here, let me show you another trick."

He placed one finger on my chest...and pushed. I'm sorry to report . . .

PLOP.

Okay, we've got some business to take care of. That passage you just read contains some . . . uh . . . very secret, highly classified information about our . . . uh . . . security systems. If that information ever leaked out to enemy spy organizations, it could have very serious consequences.

So I'm sure you'll agree that we need to do something about that, right? Of course you do. I would appreciate it if you would repeat the following Solemn Oath of Secrecy. Raise your right hand and repeat the oath:

"I, (your name), do solemnly swear that I probably didn't read the passage I just read, but if I did, I don't remember one thing about it. In the unlikely event that I remember a few details, I understand that they were based on rumors and gossip, and I refuse to believe that Hank the Cowdog would get sandbagged by a monkey."

There! I feel better now. I hate to put you under oath, but you must understand that dogs in high positions sometimes have to . . . well, protect our little reader-friends from false impressions. See, we have your best interests at heart, we really do, and, gosh, wouldn't we feel bad if you got the wrong idea? Ha ha. Sure we would.

Anyway, we're going to forget that last scene and mush on with the story. It was night, remember? Slim Chance had fallen asleep in the bathtub, and I was out there on Life's Front Lines, expecting that the ranch would be struck by a gang of monkey burglars.

Ha ha. Would you believe that *nothing happened*? No kidding. I mean, it seems funny now, that I got myself all worked up and worried over nothing. Ha ha. But nothing happened and nobody came.

In fact, it turned out to be a pretty boring night, and sometime around ten o'clock, I just, you know, went to bed. Don't forget that I was VERY TIRED. Exhausted from a long day in the hay field. No kidding.

Anyway, that's about the end of the story. We never heard another word about the monkey burglars and . . . well, everything turned out peachy keen. So you can put this book away and go brush your teeth or something, and I'll see you down the . . .

Wait. Stop. Hold everything. Don't close your book. There's something I haven't told you.

Sigh.

Sit down and take a deep seat. This is liable to come as a terrible shock. I didn't want to tell you this, but maybe I should.

Here's the deal. In that last scene, did you notice that my speech started getting slurred? Well, there's a reason for that. See, you probably thought that Lucy was a sweet, innocent little monkey girl who had been led down the wrong path by a villain named Willie, right?

Ha! What a joke. Lucy was a sweet, innocent little CROOK, only she wasn't sweet or innocent, and she wasn't even a girl. She was Bub, wearing a phony disguise and...well, maybe you've already figured that out.

Anyway, she was Bub, and he gave me two pieces of candy that were loaded with a deadly poison from the jungles of Mamby Pamby. He *slipped me a mickey*, is what he did, and he sure didn't do it by accident.

There it is, the dreadful truth. Now you know.

Did I survive the Poisoning Episode? To find out, you'll have to keep on reading.

CHAPTER TWELVE

Ruined, Disgraced, a Dismal Failure

Fellers, I had been ambushed, and I never saw it coming. Not only had I fallen for the Lucy disguise, but I had eaten the doctored candy—two pieces! I mean, hadn't I heard Deputy Kile say that they used tranquilizers on dogs? Yes, I'd heard it. I'd had plenty of warning, yet somehow . . .

I can't even describe how stupid I felt.

When I woke up, it was broad daylight and I was sprawled across the gravel drive in front of the machine shed like . . . something. Like a cuckoo clock that had been pitched out of a speeding car, and we're talking about gears and wheels and springs spread out over half an acre.

That's exactly how I felt, like a busted clock. And you talk about headache! Obviously the

117

deadly poison had worked its mischief on my head, and I was just lucky to have lived through the night.

But the worst part of waking up was that two scowling men stood over me. I blinked my eyes, jacked myself up onto four sloshy legs, and finally figured out who they were. Slim and Deputy Kile.

Deputy Kile held a little notebook in his hand. "So they tranquilized your dog. Where were you when it happened?"

"I ain't telling."

"Slim, I need to know."

"Can you keep it out of your report?"

"Maybe. We'll see."

Slim gazed off in the distance. "I fell asleep in the dadgum bathtub."

Deputy Kile looked up from his notebook, stared at Slim for a moment, and broke out laughing. "You fell asleep in the bathtub?"

Slim looked miserable. He dug his hands into his pockets and kicked a rock. "Heck yes, and didn't wake up till seven o'clock this morning. I've got dishpan hands all over my body." He looked down at me. "At least Hank had a good excuse. My only excuse is that I seem to fall asleep at all the wrong times. And I'm dumber than dirt." He shot a glance at Deputy Kile. "But that don't need to go in your report."

He smiled. "What did they take?"

"Everything that wasn't nailed down, every stinking tool on the ranch. They picked us clean as a goose, and Loper's going to cook what's left of my goose when he finds out. Any chance we can get the tools back?"

Deputy Kile wrote something down and slipped the notebook into his pocket. "We never give up on a case, but this guy's a smart cookie. My guess is that he's left the county and maybe the state. We'll do what we can." He gave Slim a pat on the shoulder. "Cheer up, buddy, and look at the bright side. They didn't steal your dog."

Laughing at his own joke (I didn't see the humor of it myself), Deputy Kile climbed into his car and drove away. Slim heaved a heavy sigh and dug his hands deeper into his pockets.

"Well, I guess I'd better start looking for another job. Maybe they need somebody to sweep out the pool hall."

Yes, and maybe I needed to start looking around for another job too. I mean, I could already imagine what Loper would say when he heard that I had let a scheming little monkey rob us blind.

Slim and I would be court-martialed, stripped

of all rank and pay, fired, thrown out on the street. And you know what? We deserved it. There wasn't a ranch in Texas that needed a hired hand who slept all the time, or a guard dog that was dumb enough to . . .

You know what really hurt about this deal? I had relaxed my guard and had allowed a cynical, conniving little monkey to use my decent impulses against me. I mean, he'd played me like a puppet on a violin.

Remember when Bub said he hated his job? Ha! HE LOVED HIS JOB. He was born to be a crook, a liar, an impostor. He loved to steal and rob, and most of all, he loved slipping mickeys to guard dogs who thought they were too smart to get fooled by a monkey.

That was a perfect description of ME, and it made me sick.

The day started out bleak and got bleaker. Slim unloaded the rest of the hay in the stack lot and did some patching on a section of barbed-wire fence, but I could see that his heart wasn't in it. The light had gone out of his eyes, and he dragged himself through his chores like a scarecrow.

I followed around behind him, carrying my own share of burdens. We were a sad pair, Slim and I. I don't know where Drover went during all of this, but he just vanished without a trace.

The last thing in the world Slim wanted to do that day was take Miss Viola to the dance at Lipscomb, but he had promised. We quit work around five and drove down to Slim's shack. He cleaned up and changed clothes, and when he came outside, I was waiting on the porch.

Our eyes met, and he said, "It hurts, don't it?"

Yes, more than I could express.

"You want to go to Lipscomb?"

Actually, I couldn't think of anything I wanted to do, but going to Lipscomb might be better than brooding all night on the porch. Sure.

"You'll have to ride in the back. I don't want you stinking up the cab for Viola."

I didn't care. I no longer felt worthy of Miss Viola's love, and I didn't have any desire to argue about my smell.

We picked up Viola at her parents' house down the creek. In the voice of a beaten man, Slim told her the whole story. She didn't say much, just nodded and gave him a pat on the arm.

It was a long, silent thirty-mile drive to Lipscomb, a tiny village that consisted of a few stores on the town square, and maybe fifty houses. We parked on the square, and Slim and Viola got

out.

Viola said, "Try to cheer up. Let's dance and have a little fun."

"I'll try," Slim said, but he was so lost in dark thoughts that he didn't even tell me to stay in the back of the pickup.

They walked across the street to the out-door dance platform, where dozens of couples were waltzing and two-stepping to Frankie McWhorter's fiddle music. Viola took Slim by the arm and dragged him onto the dance floor, and they vanished into the crowd.

I curled up in the back of the pickup and tried to lose myself in sleep, but the sounds of music and laughter kept me awake. I stood up and looked around. Well, I might as well take a walk and check out the sights of downtown Lipscomb. Moping in the back of the pickup wasn't going to change anything.

I'd heard it said that Lipscomb had more wild turkeys than people, but tonight it was hopping, filled with country folks who'd come to town for the big dance. I was walking down the street, trying to avoid getting stepped on, when suddenly I stopped dead in my tracks.

On the wooden porch in front of Beeson's Saddle Shop, I saw a *monkey* dancing the Texas Two-Step in front of a crowd of people. He was dressed in a cute little cowboy costume and held out a tin cup, as he moved his bare feet in time with "San Antonio Rose." The crowd laughed and clapped and dropped money into the cup.

A *monkey*? On an average weekend in the Texas Panhandle, how many monkeys could you expect to see? Not many. All at once, I felt myself becoming very suspicious. I moved in for a closer look.

My gaze swept across the crowd until I found the missing piece of the puzzle. Almost invisible, standing in the shadows on the edge of the crowd, a tall man with cold dark eyes watched the show. He observed it all with a silent smirk.

Willie.

We had our man, right there in downtown Lipscomb! And I had to get the word to Slim!

I raced down the street toward the dance platform, darting between legs and dodging the feet of strolling couples. I had reached the steps leading up to the dance floor, when someone reached out and grabbed me.

"Hey, pooch, you can't go up there!"

I looked around and saw that . . . yipes . . . I had just been nabbed by Deputy Kile!

I didn't want to show any disrespect for the law, but I was on a very important mission, and I didn't have time to explain it. He tried to hold me back, but I fought and struggled and finally broke out of his grasp. I raced up the steps and . . . ouch! . . . got trampled by a pair of cowboy boots.

The dance floor was packed with dancers. I ran my gaze over the crowd and saw dozens of people, old, young, and in between: a gray-headed man dancing with his granddaughter, an elderly lady creeping along in the arms of a handsome cowboy, a young mother and dad two-stepping with a baby in their arms.

I would never find Slim in this crowd! It was hopeless. I turned and was about to leave, when I heard a voice above me. "Hank, get back in the pickup." I lifted my eyes and looked into the faces of Slim and Viola. He nudged me with his boot. "Go on. You can't stay here."

There are times in a dog's life when he absolutely MUST communicate a message to his people. Most of the time, it doesn't matter. They don't listen to us and we don't always pay attention to them, and we just bungle along while our words pass one another like fishing bobbers in the night.

But this time it mattered. I looked him straight in the eyes and gave him a bark that contained an edge of urgency. "Slim, we spend a lot of time goofing off, but this time it's different. I've got something to show you, and you have to trust me."

I searched his face and held my breath. He scowled and started to say something, but Viola spoke first. "Slim, let's take a walk. I need some fresh air."

Had she understood my message? I don't know, but she'd made the right call. They left the dance floor and made their way toward the street. I went in front of them, pointing the way and trying to keep my savage impulses under control.

Once we'd gotten Slim moving in the right direction, everything else fell into place pretty quickly. When he saw the dancing monkey, he knew what he was looking at. His eyes darted around until he spotted Willie, still lurking in the shadows and looking suspicious. "It's them," Slim whispered, and walked a hundred feet to the east, where Deputy Kile was eating a bowl of homemade ice cream with his wife.

Slim whispered something in his ear. The deputy set his bowl of ice cream down on a wooden bench, pulled a two-way radio off his belt, and made a call. Five minutes later, a deputy sheriff's car pulled up in front of the saddle shop. The two officers walked over to a very surprised Willie and eased him off to the side.

When they opened up the camper and shined flashlights inside, they found every tool he'd robbed from our ranch, from Viola's place, and from several other farms and ranches in the area. While the officers loaded Willie into the backseat of the deputy's car, I walked over to Bub, who was wearing handcuffs and waiting his turn.

He was surprised to see me. "You!"

"Hi, Bub. Well, you were right about one thing. Being a thief is degrading. I don't think your

mother would be proud of you tonight."

He curled his lips into an ugly sneer. "Yeah? Well, how would your old lady feel about you being a dumbbell, huh? Get used to it, big shot, I made a monkey out of you!"

I waited for his laughter to fade out. Then I leaned forward and whispered, "You got it wrong, Bub. The monkey's the one who gets sent to the zoo. Have a nice day, you little creep."

And that's about all the story. The next afternoon around four, Loper and Sally May returned from their vacation. When Slim asked if they'd had fun, Loper said, "Oh, you bet. Alfred caught a couple of high-class trout. I figure they cost me about five hundred bucks apiece. How'd it go here at the ranch?"

Slim shrugged. "Oh, just normal." He looked down at me and gave me a wink. "We hauled a little hay and patched up some fence. Same old stuff."

Slim never said a word about napping under the truck or falling asleep in the bathtub, and I knew better than to open my mouth. That story will go with us to our graves.

Case cl—

Wait. There's one little problem. Let's try to . . . you know, keep this story to ourselves, what do you say? Don't forget that you swore a solemn oath.

Thanks. Oh, and that Lucy business? Ha ha. Look, I never really fell for that disguise, not a hundred percent. No kidding.

Case closed.

The following activities are samples from *The Hank Times*, the official newspaper of Hank's Security Force. Please do not write on these pages unless this is your book. Even then, why not just find a scrap of paper?

For more games and activities like these, as well as up-to-date news about upcoming Hank books, be sure to check out Hank's official website at **www.hankthecowdog.com**!

"Photogenic" Memory Quiz

W e all know that Hank has a "photogenic" memory—being aware of your surroundings is an important quality for a Head of Ranch Security. Now you can test your powers of observation.

How good is your memory? Look at the illustration on page 5 and try to remember as many things about it as possible. Then turn back to this page and see how many questions you can answer.

1. Was the jack on the bumper standing up straight, leaning left, or leaning right?

2. How many tires were there? 0, 1, or 2?

3. Was Deputy Kile sitting on a tire, or a bucket, or a stool?

4. Could you see Hank's tail?

5. How many of Deputy Kile's hands could you see? 1, 2, 3, or 5?

Eye-Crosserosis

I've done it again. I was staring at the end of my nose and had my eyes crossed for a long time. And you know what? They got hung up—my eyes, I mean. I couldn't get them uncrossed. It's a serious condition called Eye-Crosserosis. (You can read what big problems Eye-Crosserosis cost me in my second book.) This condition throws everything out of focus, as you can see. Could you help me turn the double letters and word groupings below into words?

~~OO~~	MM	**1.**	SUER _____	**7.**	JEYFISH _____	
PP	EE	**2.**	CKIE _____	**8.**	GUEED _____	
TT	LL	**3.**	RAIT _____	**9.**	PINEALE _____	
SS	ZZ	**4.**	BOOM _____	**10.**	SPCH _____	
RR	BB	**5.**	SWT _____	**11.**	AOW _____	
EE	OO	**6.**	RSTER <u>ROOSTER</u>	**12.**	FIY _____	

Answers:

1. SUMMER   4. BOTTOM   7. JELLYFISH   10. SPEECH
2. COOKIE   5. SWEET   8. GUESSED   9. PINEAPPLE   11. ARROW
3. RABBIT   6. ROOSTER   12. FIZZY

Cowboy Decoder

Cowboy Decoding Information

	1	2	3	4	5	6
A	Y	A	O	Z	D	K
B	T	S	R	H	E	U
C	V	M	N	I	F	L

Use the cowboy decoder (above) to unscramble the following message from Slim. It was intercepted by none other than Hank.

B4 A2 C3 A6   B4 A2 C1 B5   C4

"

— — — —, — — — — —

B1 A3 C6 A5   A1 A3 B6   C6 A2 B1 B5 C6 A1

— — — — — — — — — — — — — — — —

B1 B4 A2 B1   A1 A3 B6   B2 B1 C4 C3 A6

— — — — — — — — — — — — — —?"

Have you read all
of Hank's adventures?